# ON THE RECORD

## Martin Shepard

The Permanent Press
Sag Harbor, New York 11963

Copyright© 2005 by Martin Shepard

Shepard, Martin, 1934-
On the record / by Martin Shepard
ISBN 1-57962-117-1 (alk. paper)

All rights reserved. No part of this publication or parts there of, may be reproduced in any form, except for the inclusion of brief quotes in a review without the written permission of the publisher.

THE PERMANENT PRESS
4170 Noyac Road
Sag Harbor, NY 11963

This book is dedicated to my wife Judy, who suffered through great embarrassment when I first started playing my saxophone in public, but has still stayed with me, never negated my risk-taking, and was good enough—since we both have to like a book enough to publish it under *The Permanent Press* imprint—to allow it to come out.

And to Elise, who encouraged me to proceed with this project despite my doubts about having anything worthwhile to say. I'm also indebted to her and Judy for their careful editing and suggestions.

And, lastly, to Maureen, for her unwavering support. Her interest in hearing my stories, her feedback for the writing, and her musical input were inspiring.

How blessed I am to know, to work with, and to love and be loved by these three remarkable women.

*Other available titles by Martin Shepard*

*The Do-It-Yourself Psychotherapy Book*
*DYING: A Guide for Helping and Coping*
*Fritz*
*The Reluctant Exhibitionist*
*The Seducers*

This book would not be complete without my giving
special thanks to:

**Hunky Page**, an extraordinary man and piano player who was also kind enough to score "The Music Lesson" for me.

**Andrew Baker** for his collaboration on "Mumbo Jumbo" and who made Harbor Music Studio available for recording and rerecording all of the songs on the CD.

**Jeff Mosher**, the sound engineer who did all the fine tuning.

"Today I am full of thoughts and can write what I please. I see no reason why I should not have the same thought, the same power of expression tomorrow. When I write, whilst I write, it seems the most natural thing in the world; but yesterday I saw a dreary vacuity in this direction in which now I see so much; and a month hence, I doubt not, I shall wonder who he was that wrote so many continuous pages."

Ralph Waldo Emerson, *Circles*

# ON THE RECORD

# INTRODUCTION

In 1971, when I was 37 years old, I wrote a book entitled *A Psychiatrist's Head* that was published in 1972 by *Peter Wyden*. It was a memoir concerning my work as a cutting-edge psychiatrist, my anti-Vietnam war activities, my father's death, my sex life, my use of psychedelic drugs, fatherhood, the dissolution of my marriage, and meeting Judy, my current wife.

I thought it was a bold attempt to practice what I preached as a therapist: encouraging people to be open and honest about who they were. There was some applause when the book was published, but a much greater measure of censure and unflattering gossip. Several years after its release and its going out-of-print, I was pursued by the medical authorities who cited my memoir as the reason they sought to revoke my medical license (since restored), and when I could find no publisher to reissue it, Judy and I set up *The Permanent Press* in 1978, our own publishing company, and reissued it as *Confessions Of A Defrocked Psychoanalyst* (currently in print as *The Reluctant Exhibitionist*).

Rereading it, it seems somewhat dated: the language certainly, with phrases from the '60s and '70s ("far outs" and similar words that seem like clichés today), but it proved to be a wonderful turn of events, leading me into the world of publishing which, for the past 26 years, has not only proved the most satisfying work of my life, but validated my presumption that for every door that closes, a new one opens up or, as some wise wag said when talking about buying a bad car: "If you get a lemon, make lemonade." Finding and publishing deserving works of fiction, primarily, has led to numerous honors and rewarding friendships, and working anonymously in the arts, promoting deserving writers, has provided work that still stimulates me.

A year or so ago I read a silly article in *Publishers Weekly* by a marketing person who took publishers to task for falling book sales, his recipe for success being cutting prices while spending more on advertising (a certain recipe for financial failure) and doing more creative marketing and packaging. His packaging and marketing suggestions were equally fatuous, particularly if one is doing what *The Permanent Press* was attempting. Yet something in his article placed a seed in my mind, for I was, by then, considering writing about the evolution of my own thinking over the past 34 years. I had also started writing music at the tender age of 68.

These different interests fused in February 2004, on the last day of our annual vacation in Virgin Gorda. The year before I had hooked up with a beautiful, gifted, self-taught musician, Marcus Mark, who arranged, played back-up, and recorded my first song, *Serenity*, having to do with what is worth seeking in life. On this current trip—after writing and recording a pre-Iraqi invasion antiwar song with friends and neighbors in Sag Harbor, *Mumbo Jumbo*—I worked with Marcus on four more compositions.

Driving to the ferry returning to St. Thomas, where we would catch our flight to New York, I smoked a joint Marcus had given me earlier. That's when the notion of *On The Record* came to me; an attempt to integrate words and song; to write and publish a book, where prose and a music CD would work to augment one another in complementary fashion.

It's odd in a way, that smoking dope would spark this project, for my daily ration of marijuana in my thirties has long since disappeared. When I smoked then it was to take the edge away from being overly focused; an attempt to let my mind roam freely and unanchored. But writing this at the age of 69, the years have already brought about an unfocused mind of its own accord, and I'm not particularly interested in floating free of my already declining attention span. If I get high four times a year, usually with a younger friend or family member as an act of bonding, it's sufficient. Yet I remember the high I experienced when writing a novel in my late thirties, *The Seducers*. Then, "under the influence," the dialogue and plot came pouring out of me, without thought, as a complete surprise and all I could do was hope to write down the lines that appeared uninvited. It was the sort of high one gets when improvising musically, when things are at their best, and you feel you are not playing the music but the music is playing you. It's one of the reasons that jazz is my favorite form of music: you start off with a theme and you close with it, but in between the opening and the ending, you can sail off into, and explore, unexpected territory.

I can only hope that some of that magic still remains, and that these words can flow unrehearsed, just as the accompanying songs first came to me.

*Martin Shepard, January 2005*

# THE MUSIC LESSON

***The Music Lesson*** *was recorded at Harbor Music Studio, Sag Harbor, New York, in August, 2004, Bruce Dinsmore, on the keyboard, accompanying my saxophone.*

# THE MUSIC LESSON

When I was 9 years old I wanted to play the trumpet. My parents would have none of it and offered piano lessons instead. They felt it was a quieter instrument and easier on their ears than listening to a child honking loudly on a horn. Piano and violin were the instruments of choice in my parents' generation and besides which, my mother's sister Betty taught piano. So I would take lessons from her.

The upright they bought was fun at first: a keyboard to pick out notes, pound, and create a melody, however unmelodious it might have sounded to others. But then the lessons started. Scales, Czerny's exercises, Beethoven's *Fur Elise*. And practicing for an hour after school every day when my friends were playing stickball outside. It soon grew both burdensome and boring, and after a year or two I gave it up.

Next, as a 12 year old, I took a fancy to the guitar. Les Paul was popularizing the instrument on the airways, folk songs were plucked and strummed by counselors at camp, and records by Burl Ives and Richard Dyer Bennet were played on the radio and on phonographs. Here, too, approaching some new "toy" with which to make sounds was appealing. But again, in short order, lessons and work dulled the initial excitement. After guitar, I had an even briefer affair with an accordion, which my Dad took up in his middle years. By the time I entered late adolescence and started college I was a listener, not a player. The players I listened to live, at Birdland and Basin Street and the Five Spot—Miles Davis, John Coltrane, Dave Brubeck,

George Shearing, Johnny Smith, J.J. Johnson and Kai Winding, Chet Baker, and Gerry Mulligan—were a joy to both hear and to see. They also set an impossible standard to live up to. Why even attempt to play an instrument when it could never measure up to what these guys could create? Better to listen to the greats than make prosaic music myself.

I didn't get back into music as a player again until I was in my mid thirties. It was in the late '60s, and the Woodstock generation was coming on strong. I was working as a psychiatrist and, like others, challenging authority and the establishment, opposing the war in Vietnam, making love not war, trying to work through jealousy and possessiveness, living an open marriage, smoking a lot of marijuana and taking copious amounts of stronger psychedelics. Among the cultural distractions at that time were clubs in which the patrons took of their clothes, changed to a toga, sat on platforms where stage smoke arose from the floor, and were given cymbals, tambourines, small drums, wood flutes, and, under the influence of marijuana, all were encouraged to play them.

It was a revelation. This roomful of total strangers established a beat, got into a groove, and began to make music together. The joy of playing returned, and I fell in love with a tambourine. From that it was on to drums—conga, quinto, tumba, and African hand drums. Later on we would get together with neighbors in Bridgehampton for covered dish dinners, music making and dancing once a week. "Drumming and dancing," we all called it, but other instruments were brought in as well. I purchased a keyboard and banged on that for a while. One evening I borrowed a saxophone from a friend who brought one over. I had no knowledge of what I was doing, other than putting the reed end in my mouth and blowing. The thrill of being able to make large sounds on this horn, and the pleasure of blowing through the mouthpiece was exhilarating. Almost instantly the sax became my instrument of choice.

In sports, one can be a player or a spectator. The same two possibilities exist with music. As a listener ("spectator"), you turn on the radio or a CD, or go to a concert. Spectatorship is an easy choice. Being a player in either music or sports involves more active participation, but the results are equally, if not more rewarding and enduring, for you are developing skills, testing limits, fine tuning, and exercising your body.

All of us listen to music, yet too few appreciate the joys of being a player. The root cause of this is the same as the reason our educational system functions so poorly. Traditional "Music Lessons," like traditional curriculum in most primary and secondary schools, have the effect of taking much of the joy—and discovery—out of the process, for they begin by emphasizing *studying*: learning exercises, reading music, and practicing scales. This means a child has to "work" at music from the very beginning, instead of "playing" with it. Too often this kills the spirit.

Another factor in minimizing musical participation is the fear of embarrassment; not wanting to try playing in front of others for fear of criticism, of not "measuring up," of hitting wrong notes, of being teased or laughed at. What a shortsighted, though culturally prevalent, fear this is! How different so-called "primitive societies" are, where members of the tribe all make music together—both children and adults—without derision. To my way of thinking they relate to music in a more advanced and sophisticated way than we do.

Attending one of Jamie Aebersold's jazz workshops in my early sixties a few years back, the great saxophone player James Moody, a very down-to-earth, funny, and compassionate guy, was talking about practicing. When he would walk down the halls past practice rooms everyone was trying to impress, so rather than make errors they were trying to strut their stuff. "So I told them, 'Practicing should sound like shit. If it doesn't sound like shit, you ain't practicing'." In other words, to get somewhere, try and check your ego at the door. Even from the very beginning. "Don't you think that when Charlie Parker first started playing, he sounded like shit, too? Everyone does. You only get better by doing it. The more you do it, the better you get, and that's just the way it goes."

Phil Woods, another gifted saxophonist, approached it differently when someone asked him why he practiced so much. "I'm not practicing, I'm playing," he answered.

I came to learn these things first hand. It was alright playing a saxophone with neighbors and friends at drumming and dancing sessions. After all, it was all fun and games, I was stoned, others were too, or tipsy from wine, and everyone was in the same boat, musically speaking. One night Jerome Robbins came by to one of these music session and when he left he said what fun it had been. All of this was affirming. Still, once I began to commit myself to music, I went through these very same inhibitions.

When, years later, I realized I could make myself practice daily, I dared to take some saxophone lessons with another Sag Harborite, Hal McKusick, someone I was hesitant to approach, for I had heard jazz recordings of Hal's when I was in my twenties and felt intimidated by his expertise. Soon, however, I realized that my fears were unfounded and that to learn more I had to do it without getting high.

Committing myself meant putting the horn in my mouth every day and blowing. But what to do when I was traveling, going on vacations, exhibiting at book fairs in Frankfurt or London or the United States? To get up the nerve to play in public when nobody else was playing with me, I'd often sneak off and smoke a joint to get high first, to lessen my self-consciousness. Then, playing as softly as I could during exhibition hours to get my time in, I would encounter various reactions: some complaints ("lower the noise"... or "here's a dollar; put it toward taking some lessons first") as well as Judy's walking away from our booth when I started to tootle, for she thought it sounded so awful. "Why are you doing this," other folks asked, "to attract attention?" "No," I'd answer honestly "I'm just committed to practicing and this is the only time in the day I can do it."

Still, there were also encouraging encounters which included meeting some very nice people who, intrigued, came by to listen, chat, or give a thumbs up. These included Dr. Ruth, who walked by one year, gave me one of her impish grins, and dropped some coins into the bell of my saxophone. This acceptance provided me with enough support so that I didn't pack it in abruptly and give the whole thing up.

There were other highlights as well. One was meeting Archie Moore, the former light-heavyweight champion who fought for an incredible 27 years and knocked out more opponents—141 of them—than anyone else in the history of boxing. Archie was promoting his own book at The American Booksellers Convention in a booth adjacent to ours, and after I finished practicing he told me he dug the music. We wound up chatting about musicians we both admired, John Coltrane and Miles Davis being at the top of both our all-star lists. But the grandest memory of all had to be my encounter with Margaret Thatcher years ago at a Booksellers Convention in the States.

This was the situation: Thatcher was brought over by her publisher to promote her memoir and was scheduled to enter our hall in mid-afternoon to do a book signing. Our booth was in the aisle that led from the hall entrance to the signing area. Earlier that morning, on another floor, I had passed the exhibit of a major publisher who was promoting a book about the royal family and, to draw attention to it, had life sized stand-up cutouts of Prince Charles, The Queen, and Princess Diana. This series of coincidental events was too good to be ignored and presented a great opportunity for merriment.

Prior to "The Iron Lady's" entrance I borrowed the members of the Royal Family and stood them up in front of our small booth. Judy, in her fashion, decided to walk away before my impromptu performance. At the appointed hour, the exhibition doors opened, there was a hush of expectations, and Thatcher made her entrance as I began to play *God Save the Queen*. Had a cameraman been there, he would have witnessed a scene out of *Fawlty Towers*, with John Cleese playing a saxophone surrounded by cardboard royalty. Except that Cleese, in his sitcom role, would have been hoping to impress the most powerful woman in the world, whereas I was just trying to have some fun with the situation. My problem was in trying to suppress laughter, and nothing is more difficult than playing a horn if your lips are quivering with anticipated mirth. Fortunately—like a man having intercourse who thinks about baseball or car repairs in order to gain control over a premature orgasm—I was able to divert attention sufficiently and continue. When, finally, Margaret reached our stand, her entire procession of a dozen or more people paused from their military/security style march and stopped literally in their tracks. Margaret turned to face me, raised her eyebrows, flashed me a beautiful smile, nodded appreciatively, and told me with her long vowel, upper class British accent "How looovely! Simply looovely!" It was all I could do to continue blowing as she departed, and when I concluded the last stanza there was applause from the other exhibitors who were watching and aware of my plan. Then we just about rolled in the aisle, grinning, laughing foolishly, and high-fiving one another.

All of this stubbornness, this refusal to give in to my own self-consciousness, was what allowed me to keep playing and to use music as my own form of yoga. I would recommend this attitude to anyone else who wants to enjoy the benefit of song as a type of salvation, who wants to learn an instrument, or play for the pure pleasure of it.

If infants were embarrassed because their initial attempts to talk came out wrong, they would stop trying and never learn to speak. Should not the same tolerance hold for musical expression as it does for verbal expression? Music after all, at its best, is a way to converse with people without speaking, and in many instances, to converse on a deeper level. People who speak different languages or whose intellectual preoccupations vary tremendously can experience the joy of harmonious and creative interaction by "talking" to one another through their instruments, creating a non-verbal dialogue that expresses and shares emotion simply through playing with one another.

I'm sure you've heard music that has made you cry out

of joy or sorrow, or powerfully recalled events in your past life that touched your heart after hearing just a few notes, songs that make you want to jump up and dance, recollect love lost or found, and remember moments you shared with friends, parents or children. Barry White's *Let the Music Play* always makes me want to dance and I am back in my thirties, when I twirled and whirled to his lush, sensual sounds. Dylan's *Mr. Tambourine Man* (as well as Abbey Lincoln's soulful, jazzy interpretation of his tune) brings back memories of loss when, in my late thirties, my first marriage began to come apart and I grieved for the vulnerabilities of my three young sons. Nearly every song on Bill Evans' solo piano albums brings tears to my eyes, as do many plaintive, heartbreaking recordings, like Chet Baker or John Coltrane playing Robbie Williams' song *Every Time We Say Goodbye*. And I can never hear the Beatles *A Day in the Life* without reliving a phenomenal fuck in my early thirties, high on mescaline, when I climaxed at the very climactic ending of that song.

Music has a way of getting to the heart of things, emotionally speaking, even better than words.

My own evolution as a player, then, went from stoned noise making, to more sober approaches. At first, under sobriety, I would make myself practice for an hour a day—and one summer for two hours daily. Still, starting to play in my forties, and having to make a living, meant that it was too late to become the player I would have liked to be, and by my mid sixties my practice sessions eventually were cut down to 15 minutes a day and never on Sundays, a practice encouraged by another of my Aebersold teachers, who said that "playing for even five minutes a day is much better than forcing yourself to play for an hour and resenting the time." This schedule worked well, particularly when melodies began to come to me.

Song writing started like this:

I was reading *The New York Times*, which was propped up on my music stand, blowing away mindlessly, when my attention slipped from the sports page to the sounds coming out of my horn. "Hummnn. Those are some interesting notes," I thought. "I think I'll write them down." This writing down of serendipitous sounds is what led to song-writing, for having happenstance notes written on paper meant I could work on them over and over again, adding, subtracting, until I had a tune. Then, when I composed my first melody, came the second problem: writing lyrics. What sort of lyrics could I possibly write? How my girl done left me... getting drunk in a bar... singing the blues... writing rap... being friendless and loveless? My life has been pretty stable and serene for years now and, though I've enjoyed listening to songs like that, none of these situations were relevant to my experiences. Trying to be imitative would be both pointless and silly. So what did I have to say?

And then it hit me. I'd been a psychiatrist, a student of Buddhism and Taoism, been married twice, had three kids and three step-kids. There were also many work experiences. In my youth I was a shipping clerk, drove an ice-cream truck (I was a Bungalow Bar man) and a UPS truck in New York's garment center, operated an elevator at a downtown Manhattan department store for women, and bused and waited tables. Later on, aside from my political activism, I earned a living as a doctor, a psychiatrist, an author, a home designer and builder, and, finally as a publisher. It was these experiences, coupled with the attitudes that accompanied them, that would serve as a source for lyrics on any tunes I wanted to add words to.

Between 2003 and 2004 seven songs came, uninvited, to me. For this chapter, "the last shall be first." *The Music Lesson*, with no lyrics at all, arose from a series of notes that reminded me of those endless Czerny exercises that all budding piano students are forced to practice. Fittingly enough, for the lead-in I chose a metronome.

# SERENITY

## SERENITY

Since life delivers joy and sorrow
Here today and gone tomorrow
Is there any recipe for dealing with its pain?

Self-absorption's not the answer
Cultivate both love and laughter
Know that sunshine always follows rain.

Rid yourself of all expectations
Take things as they come
Try to see the world through other's eyes.

Work at things that give you pleasure
Share your secret dreams
Toss away the ties that bind you
So that your destiny might find you.

Health and wealth are insufficient
If your values are deficient
Serenity is all you need to lead a blissful life.

Your time's too short for fears or sorrow
Live as though there's no tomorrow
And serenity will fill your life.

# SERENITY

What is the ultimate goal of human life? What is it we're striving for? It depends, I suppose, to whom you put this question and at what point in their life you ask. Reflecting on my life, I remember early goals. As a child there were nightly prayers, done in private at the side of my bed:

"Now I lay me down to sleep
I pray the Lord my soul to keep
If I should die before I wake
I pray the Lord my soul to take."

From ages 5 to 12, it's clear that my answer would have been "To keep on living." Monsters, goblins, murderers might be anywhere and the thought of dying was terrifying.

From 12 to 19, after discovering my penis could give pleasure far beyond that afforded by urinating, my basic goal shifted. Now my fervent prayers were that I would have the experience of fucking before dying. Lesser goals might have been to be more popular and be more self-assured.

From 20 on there were other goals: to become a doctor...to find someone to love who would love me back...to be financially successful...to be happy...to be less inhibited.

Some time in my forties I was asked what I would wish for if I had only one wish, and the word that popped out of my mouth was "Serenity." Since then, when toasting with both friends and strangers, it's what I always hold highest. When others toast to "Health" or "Happiness" or "Love," I always toast to "Serenity." I've come to see it as the ultimate prize, for if you have serenity, you can sail through any of the obstacles and challenges that life will invariably offer. Money, accomplishments, health, sex mean nothing if you are anxious, fearful, tense, and worried. Poverty, sickness, and loss cause no psychic pain if you are serene. It's the Buddha state of mind, a state of bliss, of contentedness; a state of acceptance, of unhurriedness, of just being "present and appreciative" as the world goes by.

I believe that everyone is on a quest for serenity, whether they articulate it or not. It's one of the reasons why Buddhism became so popular in America, for it attempts nothing less than trying to deliver to its adherents this very special state of mind. Listening to, or looking at the relaxed, whimsical, smiling, compassionate repose of the Dalai Lama, is it any wonder that he is often referred to as "His Serene Excellency?"

The big question, of course, is how does one achieve serenity? The Buddha said that desire creates pain. Give up desires and you give up pain. There is no question that unmet desires are the cause of much suffering, and while I've been able to give up some of them, I still have lots of desires left in my backpack. Zen practitioners utilize meditation as a way of finding this peaceful state. They sit in a lotus position, concentrate on their respiration or focus on some object, put thoughts out of their minds, and enter a state of tranquility, where they can let go of all the muscular tensions in their bodies. From there they hope to simply enjoy breathing and going nowhere, entering the timelessness of eternity while still being very present.

I've played with meditation techniques in years past, but they did not yield much of a payoff for me. Sitting was uncomfortable, offering only limited muscular relaxation. Like learning golf, I didn't feel I wanted to put in the time and effort this technique required. I was looking to find a greater serenity through less effort and less work.

Serenity is, when all is said and done, a state of grace, and many have reportedly gotten there through traditional religious faith and studies. That path, however, did not do it for me either. I've seen too many people who regularly attend services at churches, synagogues, and mosques, as well as various ministers, rabbis and ayatollahs who fail to display the characteristics of being at peace with the world and themselves.

My father's father and my father were atheists. My mother's parents were orthodox Jews. In my parents' marriage, my dad's lineage was the dominant influence. I grew up in a neighborhood that was not segregated by religion. Christian families went to services at their churches, Jewish families went to services at synagogues, and our family went nowhere at all. Being brought up in a secular way, belonging to no sect, and not fitting in with any religious tribes made me feel out of place. Now I consider this background among my blessings.

On the Jewish High Holy Days, when I was young, my folks would take my sister and me to visit my mom's parents. In attendance at these Passover meals were my mother's three sisters and their children. I remember vividly the sort of conversations the adults in my mother's family would hold, discussing, among other things, how my cousin Carol was marrying a "goy," and her brother was marrying a "shiksa." And they would talk about the "schvartzes"—the blacks. I found it all so unappealing. Here were these Jews who felt that they were a people who were discriminated against, yapping in the most discriminatory way about Christians and black people. It struck me as both hypocritical and absurd, and made me glad that I was not a card-carrying member of the "Faith." Because of these experiences I've never considered myself to be a Jew any more than I considered myself to be a Cleveland Indians fan; no offense to the followers of either of these of these culturally recognized cults.

When someone asks if I am Jewish, I never know what to answer, for I consider that a "Yes" response means that you follow Jewish religious principles. If the is answer "No," one gets accused of *Denial*. To me, most formal religions are divisive, clubby affairs, like fraternities on campus, or the special clubs kids form in grade schools to separate "us," the chosen people, from "them," the less deserving. My usual response is to roll my eyes, shrug my shoulders, or ask what they mean by that question.

My religious beliefs are relatively simple: that we are all interconnected with one another and with the physical world we live in, and that harmony is far better than divisiveness. This is Buddhist thought without taking out membership in any Buddhist sect. It also is clear to me that no one will ever achieve serenity without starting with these basic assumptions. So-called Holy Men, as well as politicians, and ordinary citizens, who promote divisiveness, who believe that gays should not be allowed to marry, that Jews should subdue Palestinians or that Arabs should subdue Jews, or that Serbs should dominate Bosnians, etcetera, are not models of serene human beings. I see them, instead, as opportunistic, angry, judgmental, or ignorant people; people I try to avoid. I can't believe the words of those who profess to believe in the "Right to Life" of a fetus, but will be among the first to wave their respective flags and support wars that kill adults.

The established religions—better referred to as the Establishment Religions—in this country are far less than two dozen, and are akin to major league baseball franchises, with perhaps 16 teams having franchises and gaining special privileges like tax exemptions (and, lately, federal funding), and having a "respected" place at the table of Public Opinion. Whereas spiritual people who are not organized as Roman Catholics, Greek or Russian Orthodox, Presbyterians, Episcopalians, Baptists, Mormons, Muslims, reformed and conservative and orthodox Jews, Seventh Day Adventists, Jehovah's Witnesses, Quakers,etcetera are not taken seriously but are, instead, marginalized.

While I do not believe in a personal God, I do give thanks for all my blessings. I do know that I consider many of my closest friends to be spiritual people, though they are not members of any particular sect. They are people like me who don't want to join exclusive groups or feel the need for formal, sanctioned, or ritualistic prayer. A majority of the individuals I cherish are members of this same tribe-less, leaderless tribe, and it's very easy to recognize them. To paraphrase Howard Dean, a former presidential candidate, "We represent the Spiritual Wing of the Unaffiliated Religious Party." In fact, I suspect that we are the true SILENT MAJORITY, though we've never organized in a political sense so that neither the media nor politicians take note of us. When incumbents or candidates of all political stripes periodically trot off to church in order to impress the "Organized Religious" electorate with their spirituality, they don't impress any of us. When they talk about "religious values," they are not necessarily talking about our religious values. If they want to play to our concerns, they'd have to curb their inclinations to exert power over others and their enthusiasm to make wars and address, instead, their neglect of the poor. They'd have to share the wealth, respect the fragility of the earth that sustains us, and stop despoiling it.

We are all citizens of planet earth, and this should be our basic allegiance, for our fates are interdependent. We should not place allegiances of any sort above this, including national allegiances, for that is the road to conflict. I'm for rejecting a patriotism that quotes Patrick Henry's "I regret that I have but one life to *give* for my country" and, instead, embrace the notion that "I welcome the fact that I have one life to *live* for this world."

One can readily say this about people who have serenity: they accept life's flow and don't insist on trying to make events conform to their wishes. The ancient Greeks talked about "destiny," a concept that is not honored as much today as it once was. One might speculate that those living lives of quiet desperation, of frustration, or of tedious routines are living out their destinies. But if one were to define destiny differently, as the full realization of what they are capable of as human beings, I would argue that too few people fulfill their destinies. They work at jobs they don't enjoy, live in communities they don't like, and work with people they don't respect. This is often rationalized as "meeting one's responsibilities" or "being an adult," but it does not lead to peace of mind.

The "accidents" that have led me to a reasonable measure of serenity in my life started with having a loving father, a compassionate, non-judgmental man who always inspired me by example. There was also Helen Edey, a psychoanalyst at a low-cost clinic I saw while in medical school, who listened to all of my troubling inner thoughts and secrets. In the process, she allowed me to be at peace with what I thought and felt, helped me become unembarrassed about who I really was. Then there were my psychedelic experiences where, under the influence of mescaline and LSD, I had visions of my interconnectedness with Everything, which radically reduced my fear of death. These perceptions were, for me, a religious experience, but are difficult to put into words without cheapening or trivializing the effect they had on me, though I attempted to do that in both my autobiographical *The Reluctant Exhibitionist* and again in *Dying*. Today I'm less inclined to attempt explanations and more inclined to quote from Stephen Mitchell's translation of Lao Tse's *Tao te Ching*, a book I've read and reread countless times and recommend as another source of illumination. Poem 56 starts thusly:

> "Those who know don't talk
> Those who talk don't know."

Lastly, there was the companionship and love of Judy, my wife and life-partner who, over the last 34 years, has provided me with a level of comfort, peace, and understanding.

My pursuit of serenity was marked by going along with the flow of life as opposed to staying stuck in place. My mother could not understand why, though still licensed as a physician, I gave up the practice of medicine. Monotony is one answer. Another is that I fell into transitional experiences along the way that convinced me that I could support myself without a doctor's or a psychiatrist's income. While still working in the field of medicine, I began writing books and found that this provided a reasonable substitute income. One book, which is still in print, was *The Do-It-Yourself-Psychotherapy Book*. What else was there to say or do if I believed in this book—which I did and still do? It seemed pointless to keep up a practice for other than financial reasons. With Judy's encouragement (she had lived through her own financial crises when her first husband left her, but came to realize, and assure me, that "things have a way of working out"), I gave up the security of the income that flowed from being a psychiatrist. Freed from having to live near New York City, we moved to Bridgehampton, New York, in 1975, with four of our six children; two of hers and two of mine.

Moving to Long Island's East End meant expanding a summerhouse I had there, then designing a bigger one for our brood while being employed as an untrained carpenter by the builder, who was my neighbor. This led to a series of designing, building, inhabiting, and then selling other houses, which provided a richer, easier, and more stimulating life than I could possibly have had if I had remained a practicing physician. Three years later Judy and I started *The Permanent Press*, and after several years it was sufficiently profitable so that I could give up building houses and settle down to being a full time book publisher.

The lesson I learned from all these experiences was, as the tour guides say down in Disneyland "No matter where you go, there you are!" If you are competent at what you are working at now, the chances are excellent that you can be just as competent in another job or another living situation that is more nourishing to the soul, stimulating to the mind, and satisfying to the spirit, providing you are willing to abandon conventional expectations and the long-faced counsel of friends and relatives who express caution "for your own good."

Serenity requires that we find satisfaction in our work and the way we live our lives. We're so encouraged, in the course of growing up, to find a profession and practice it, that we overstay our interest and joy. Trying something new, easy for children, seems impossible for so many adults. They fear the loss of money and a style of life they've gotten hooked into. The greater the pity, for these changes are not as overwhelming as one might fear. Nor is money any compensation for boredom.

Athletes often talk of "letting the game come to you," rather than going out and trying to make things happen. When they are in that space, they refer to it as "The Zone." It's the exaltation of reacting, rather than initiating action, the comfort of being still, the admonition to "Stand there; don't just do something." This is serenity.

So do not feel imprisoned by conventional "wisdom," let the game of life come to you. Serenity, no matter what path you take to get there, comes about through letting go, not holding on, and by riding the current of your life's flow instead of swimming against circumstances.

*Serenity was recorded in Virgin Gorda in February, 2003. I sing and play saxophone: Marcus Mark did the arrangement and played everything else.*

# МИМВО JИМВО

## MUMBO JUMBO

The Ayatollah speaks of God's will
And swears jihad against infidels
He claims the people are his brothers
Except for women, girls, or mothers.
He's a Mumbo Jumbo man.

Our leader is a pious Christian
Who says he's on a Holy Mission
He wants us all to do our duty
But guarantees his friends the booty.
He's a Mumbo Jumbo man.

They set the rules for folks to live by
You make them angry and you could die
Each wants to lead us to salvation
Though it may well destroy his nation.
That's their Mumbo Jumbo plan.

Mumbo Jumbo men and women
The talking heads on television
Insecure of their positions
All support their leader's visions.
It's the Mumbo Jumbo sham.

They call upon our patriotism
And ostracize the opposition
They want to get us all on board
So they can justify their war.
That's the Mumbo Jumbo scam.

Peace means war in Mumbo Jumbo
Hate is love in Mumbo Jumbo
God is revenge in Mumbo Jumbo
The world will end with Mumbo Jumbo.

# MUMBO JUMBO

In my earlier memoir, and in my former practice of psychiatry, I made a big issue of honesty, elevating it to the top of the list of things to strive for. While still believing in the cliché that "honesty is the best policy," I think it's fair to say that as the years have passed, I've had further thoughts about it, one being that my zealotry was simple-minded, as zealotry usually is, for the issues of truth-telling and lying are a lot more complex and nuanced than the arguments I put forth in my *Do-It-Yourself Psychotherapy Book* and which formed the premise of my autobiographical memoir *The Reluctant Exhibitionist*.

Over the past 32 years I've come to appreciate the fact that lies come in all sizes and packaging. There are personal lies, committed by all of us for a variety of reasons, and there are institutional lies, the most damaging, frightening and dangerous lies of all because they tend to be of epic proportions and affect the health, lives, and safety of us all.

On a personal level I can recognize three basic categories of lies. The first being *lies of kindness*, otherwise knows as "little white lies," put forward to spare someone you care for from unnecessary hurt or pain. When a child asks a parent whom they like best—"My sister or me"—and, in fact the parent may like the sister better, but says "I like you equally," this little white lie is an act of kindness, not cowardice. If one has a jealous partner and is asked by them if you are attracted to a particular third person, and you know that an affirmative answer will cause all sorts of turmoil, a "No" might be the best response for all concerned. Or, taking it one step further, when a husband or wife denies to their mate a liaison that they know in their hearts does not threaten the marital relationship, but are also aware that the knowledge of it would deeply pain their partner, a case could be made that denial is not simply a self-serving lie, but that it is the kindest response possible.

While I am not pro- or anti- infidelity, it's worth pointing out that a significant majority of American men and women have been unfaithful to their spouse or "significant other." So it always surprises me that so many mates are shocked, depressed, or enraged when they discover that their mate has wandered, or that an indigestible, unforgivable affair is grounds for divorce, since the incidence of wandering would seem to indicate that this is a genetic predisposition, a natural state of affairs, even, perhaps, a biological necessity.

Christian Fundamentalists would argue that the prevalence of infidelity is a sign of America's moral decay. I would say that those Fundamentalists interested in the defense of marriage would be better served by opting for a Constitutional Amendment to ban infidelity as grounds for martial dissolution, instead of trying to prevent gays from marrying. One of their arguments for excluding gays from this "sacred institution" is that God intended marriage to be a union between a man and a woman formed for the purposes of procreation. Would, then, they oppose marriages between heterosexuals past the childbearing age? Or ban infertile couples from marrying? Or pass legislation to dissolve marriages if no children are born to the married couple after a period of, say, ten years? There is precedence for this in Anglo-Saxon law, for in centuries past the Kings of England could have a marriage annulled if the Queen bore no heirs.

To honor integrity concerning infidelities, one can also honestly tell one's mate in the beginning of a relationship or whenever the subject comes up ("Would you tell me if..."), that you want to reserve the right to be ambiguous: to tell or not to tell according to your own judgment. This way there is no real deception should your resolve never to stray weaken and you wanted to keep the news to yourself.

Besides lies of kindness, there are also *lies of survival*, lies told to prevent big penalties, like incarceration, or damage to the purse when one is just getting by, like paying parking tickets or income taxes when you don't feel you can afford it. A guy is bringing a few ounces of marijuana he obtained from his connection to a friend who wanted to make a purchase. It's in the glove compartment of the rental car he's driving. Stopped by the police for a traffic violation, he's ordered out of the car, his glove compartment is searched, and he is arrested. Tell the truth? Let's be real here. "I don't know anything about it, officer. It's not mine. And I want to see a lawyer as soon as you book me."

Does one expect the kid who engages in one-time shoplifting (who, in the course of growing up, has never lifted something?) to fess up and receive punishment? Not usually, despite the American myth that George Washington, as a boy, admitted to his father that he chopped down the cherry tree in their yard, when, in fact, this never occurred. When you forget to pay a credit card on time and resent getting hit with usurious late payment charges, and you call the card company and say you didn't receive the bill from them in time, "perhaps it was lost in the mail," and then, as usually happens, they agree to drop the charges for "this time only," should you tell the truth instead? As for taxes, how many citizens are scrupulously honest here? Don't most of us fudge as much as possible, overvalue contributions and fail to report as much income as we can successfully hide? Big corporations have their own loopholes written into law, and millionaires can hire expensive accountants who minimize their tax liability. Shouldn't the average citizen have some equal rights of deception here?

An old friend of mine, Vincenzo DePersis, who immigrated to America from Italy, was even bolder when he declared that "Americans feel this ridiculous sense of guilt when they cheat on their taxes when there is so much government corruption and misspending going on. In Italy everybody considers it their sacred public duty to cheat this way."

Another category of personal lies are *lies told to protect one's image*. These can be dangerous lies for they often lead one into great trouble. First of all, why bother having an image? What's wrong with just being the human being you are? As far as I'm concerned, lying to maintain an image is plain stupid.

Take the case of Martha Stewart. Her instinct to protect her image cost her far more than she bargained for. If any of us held stock, and were told by a corporate executive or a broker that the value of that stock would sink the following week because of bad developments that would soon be made public, what would we do? Sell, certainly, before the bottom fell out. But Martha had her "image," and to protect this false front of being the doyen of taste and respectability, she felt impelled to deny that she was tipped off before dumping her Imclone stock. Had she said

"Yes, I did find out about this earlier," she might have been scolded, but would not have faced jail time. She was not convicted for getting inside information, but for lying, and that was the reason for her sentencing.

The most painful case of lying to protect one's image came when Bill Clinton was asked if he had sex with Monica Lewinski. He could have said "I will answer any questions put to me about my public life, but my private life is off limits." Other than demands for full disclosure from the "Moralists," pushes by the press for a salacious news story, and howls from Clinton's right-wing political opponents, most Americans—men as well as women— would more than likely have respected that sort of response.

Succumb to the sexual advances of a younger woman? Horrors! While most guys might respond to such advances, Bill assumed that what might be a knee-jerk response from other men did not fit his image of what a President's conduct should be. So he initially denied it, and then he verbally tap-danced around the subject of what "sex" consisted of. Finally, the lies came undone. In the end it was his lying under oath that got him impeached; not the act of getting what was probably a third rate blowjob.

Clearly "My private life is none of your business" would have been Clinton's best response when the Inquisitors demanded an explanation of his sexual conduct. Had he been honest and open about what actually transpired in private with Monica, he would still have hurt and embarrassed his family and been publicly shamed, but he surely would have avoided the impeachment process. I'm familiar with sexual-shaming, for I went through that process myself, which helped make me aware of the absurdity of it all.

Once-upon-a time I thought that openness and honesty were ways to rid one's self of shame and guilt: that light cast on secrets would reveal that what we think is aberrant is really pretty human. A willingness to risk honesty, though it might offend some or disappoint others, can also free the spirit and let the world know who you are and what you stood for. I never understand how psychiatrists could proclaim that sex and lust were natural impulses, but then would never dare talk openly about their own lustful and sexual lives. This was a contradiction, one I tried to both address and reduce when I wrote *A Psychiatrist's Head*.

There was fallout, of course, along with plenty of gossip. Many within the medical/psychiatric profession saw me as a poor role model. They preferred a more wholesome image, one that insured respect; someone uncontroversial and above reproach, a non-sexual professional who wore a suit, whose judiciousness would never be called into question, and whose biological urges were sanitized by circumspection. Could I fault them for that? Not really. Reliable images of "doctor," "priest," "lawyer," "psychiatrist" are good for the professions. The discovery that there are pedophilic priests, psychiatrists who exploit patients, and physicians and lawyers whose avarice and acquisitiveness trump the needs of those they serve are bad for business.

At those points scandal and sound bites trump serious discourse. I remember a time, preceding the controversies over whether gays should be permitted in the armed forces or allowed to adopt children, when there were great debates over gay men serving as Boy Scout leaders as well as questions raised about gays being fit to teach children.

The presumption was that homosexual desires would automatically lead to exploitative behavior, a nonsensical concept when one thinks of it. Equally nonsensical is the notion that a psychiatrist who openly owns his or her own sexual life would necessarily exploit a patient.

The repercussions following the publication of *A Psychiatrist's Head* were significant. Some championed the book, but those voices were matched by others who deemed it unprofessional and outrageous. And it was those negative voices that spawned a time of trial for my family and myself. Newspaper headlines proclaiming their father a "Sex Doc," are not what children want to read or hear.

Despite this negativity, on a personal level the writing of that book was a valuable experience, for it made me realize I *could* tell anyone exactly what was on my mind. I also came to realize that this freedom might cause unnecessary hurts, and that selective honesty might be a kinder policy.

One learns only through mistakes. My first marriage fell apart, in part, because of this openness, and I was determined not to repeat that sort of experience in my second. Thus, with Judy, I decided to accept the honesty of stating we could be "ambiguous," that she or I might share stories of other loves and lusts, or might not, but no further commitment to truth was necessary.

As children we are all taught shame; shame of bodily parts and bodily functions, shame of nudity, shame of jealousy, shame of fearfulness, shame of sexual impulses, shame of honest expression, shame, in fact, of any behavior that goes against either the cultural norm or the norm in one's home. As adults we are successful to the extent that we can dispense with these shameful concepts, and a lot of the work in any psychiatric practice has to do with overcoming this mechanism that goes against one's nature, for it stifles the life force, pinching self-expression and self-acceptance. Yet shaming is a tool regularly employed by the self-appointed Morality Authorities (hardly a "Moral Majority" in my opinion, but it does have a nice ring to it) in this country. Christian Fundamentalists,* and those like George W. Bush's first Attorney General, John Ashcroft, who pander to them, are always out to police other peoples sexual lives and practices. And not just heterosexual out-of-wedlock acts but any form of homosexuality. Why else package their crusade to ban same sex marriages as "Defending the Institution of Marriage," as though there were a cabal of people (other than divorce lawyers) laying siege to it? Indeed, that gays want to get married is an affirmation of that institution, not an attack on it. Let's be frank here and face it: Christian Fundamentalists are America's Moral Police and are pushing for ever greater power to Oppose Vice and promote Virtue, just as the Taliban assumed that same role in Afghanistan before being driven from power.

*I think Christ would wince hearing the term 'Christian Fundamentalist.' I was about to say Christ would have rolled-over in his grave instead of 'winced,' but for those believing in the Resurrection it's clear that Christ ascended, leaving only his shroud behind, to join his Father and the Holy Spirit. I wonder if these Christian Fundamentalists would have approved of Christ's naked ascent into heaven; after all, in 2002, John Ashcroft spent $8,000 to drape the top nude half of *The Spirit of Justice*, a large statue that stood in the Hall of Justice, in order to cover her bare breasts.

While compassion can be extended toward those who, for better or worse, utter personal lies, I feel no compassion at all for *institutional lying*, the misleading, dishonest, distorted machinations motivated by greed or zealotry and that expose the public to great risk. If lying is a sin, it must surely be referring to this type of lie—the ultimate sin—and yet it is the one that is least punished. Why? Because institutional liars are so highly placed in society that they have partners galore: partners on interlocking boards of directors, stockbrokers and shareholders, when talking of corporate liars; and political parties as partners when we are dealing with deceptive politicians. Worse yet, these two institutions are inextricably linked together and have shown the resiliency to resist any new wave of reformers that come along.

The presidency of George W. Bush has been so filled with institutional lying that at times I feel like exploding. The worst part of all is that it came from the very top, from our President and his administration, who have made an art form of public lying. Bush's "Save our Forests" proposals were meant, of course, to let loggers infringe upon them. His "Clean Skies" initiative was designed to lower pollution standards and actually served to make our air dirtier while enriching the energy and chemical companies whose emissions continue to foul the atmosphere. His "Job Creation" tax cuts were proposed not to create jobs, but to give tax deductions to his wealthiest contributors. His "Energy Program" to create self-sufficiency was geared toward plundering the Alaskan wilderness with oil explorations, rewarding his fellow oil cronies rather than protecting the environment. But the worst lies of all were those concerning Iraq's threat to the US, its "Weapons of Mass Destruction" and fabrications that Saddam was in league with Osama bin Laden. All bullshit, all Mumbo-Jumbo.

Unlike *Serenity*, a song about how to live one's life, in which the melody came first and the lyrics second, *Mumbo Jumbo* came about because of the increasing disgust I felt when Bush relentlessly began his drive to push us into a unilateral attack on Iraq without doing it through the United Nations. I was scribbling angry verses concerning his politics (a mirror image, in many ways, of the Muslim fundamentalists he was opposing) and the free ride the media was giving him. It was then a question of creating an angry, compelling beat and tune that would carry the words, as well as putting it together with others as a community project, members of our "Tribeless Tribe"of friends and neighbors who were similarly chaffing under the abrasive and blatant misrepresentations coming out of the White House; mendacities that were readily apparent to anyone reading between the lines.

*Mumbo Jumbo* included all of the grievances I had concerning the false moralists and phony prophets on both sides of the Middle East/Western divide. The title seemed an apt synonym, for it implied certain "bait and switch" contrivances: shiftiness with a great deal of finesse, quasi-religious fervor with a rhetoric that promised salvation, though it was essentially gibberish. My 1966 edition of *Webster's New World Dictionary* had these varied definitions for mumbo jumbo, which seemed to cover the contestants in this upcoming battle between Muslim fundamentalists and our Christian Fundamentalist president:

*"1. among certain tribes a medicine man who is supposed to protect his people from evil and terrorize the women into subjection. 2. an*

*idol or fetish; hence, 3. any object of fear or dread. 4. meaningless ritual, unintelligible expression, gibberish, etc."*

I don't mean to imply here that mumbo jumbo was peculiar to the Bush administration alone. When I was in my thirties we were fed a similar line of malarkey that got us into Vietnam: a phony story put out by Lyndon Johnson's administration about a non-existent attack on a U.S. warship in the Gulf of Tonkin, which led to Congress approving the Tonkin Gulf Resolution, authorizing LBJ to involve the nation in that dirty war (with only two U.S. Senators, Wayne Morse of Oregon and William Fulbright, of Arkansas, God bless them, voting against it). At that time I was getting ever more deeply involved with the Vietnam War protest movement, participating with the Non-Violent Coordinating Committee led by the pacifist Reverend A.J. Muste and Dave Dellinger, an umbrella group that welcomed one and all, including democrats, republicans, socialists, atheists, radicals, communists... any American of any persuasion opposed to this mad escalation of the conflict. A very democratic group indeed! They accepted liberals like Bella Abzug and her Women's Strike for Peace group and even Allard Lowenstein who, on more than one occasion, wanted to oust all those radical groups to the left of him, like communists, socialists, and Trotskyites so as not to offend "mainstream" Americans; a disgraceful position as far as I was concerned. I truly believed that every American had a constitutional right to his opinion and I did not want to see another version of McCarthyism take hold. (Ironic, is it not, now that the term "liberal" is being used as a shibboleth, just as the term "red" or "pinko" or "communist" or "fellow-traveler" was used in the 1950's, so that people with left-wing persuasions have to be defensive about, or apologize for, their opinions.)

In any event, those were years of active involvement for me, with teach-ins and other active protests. I was also writing letters to draft boards, as a psychiatrist, to any anti-war person who came to me, attesting to the fact that they were mentally deranged in some way and should be deferred. This seemed fair enough, for the Johnson administration thought that any well-balanced American lad should be proud to serve his country in this war; ipso facto, if they did not want to go, they must be unsound, right? Later, myself and a friend, Ed Knappman, decided to set up a "Turn In Your War Bonds" movement after realizing what a massive amount of money was being held by our government in what used to be called "War Bonds" in the 1940's but were then sold as "Series E Savings Bonds" when World War II ended. Our reasoning was that if anti-war citizens could cause a run on the Treasury (and about 50% of Americans by then were in favor of pulling out of Vietnam), it would send a powerful message to the White House to bring the troops safely home and stop killing Vietnamese and dying themselves in a senseless war. Through mailings, phone calls, and pamphleteering we raised enough money from enough people to take out a full page advertisement in *The New York Times* that we would all sign, headed "**TURN IN YOUR WAR BONDS WEEK**" with a coupon that could be sent back to us. The ad was laid out, brought down to *The Times* and, after submission, *The Times* refused to run it, saying it "was against the national interest."

Growing up with a reverence for the *Times* (a paper that still has my respect, for I don't hold grudges well), I was aghast. "Outrageous," I thought. "We'll fight this," was my first reaction and I took the ad layout and the rejection letter from the *Times* to the American Civil Liberties Union, expecting help from that hallowed "liberal" institution. But again it was mind-boggling: they were defending the rights of Nazis to parade in Skokie, Indiana at the time and had no interest in this case. (Did I just say I don't hold grudges? Okay, I should have said I don't *usually* hold grudges, for in truth, while I still subscribe to *The New York Times* I never had any future respect for the ACLU, whose Talmudic reasoning allowed for an abstract defense of the free-speech rights of Nazis, but wouldn't lift a lawyer's finger to defend free-speech protests against a horrific war.)

Other insults were to come. Being eligible for the Doctor's draft I went down to my draft board and applied as a Conscientious Objector, and brought down letters from many people who attested to the fact that, spiritually speaking, I thought war was not a way to settle problems. Indeed, as a physician, my role was to save lives, not waste them. But being a member of The Spiritual Wing of the Unaffiliated Religious Party, they denied this request. "If you were a Quaker or a Seventh Day Adventist, you'd have a claim. But you don't participate in any Church." As said before, if you do not belong to one of the franchised religions, you have no spiritual rights when dealing with our government. Still, I eventually got off a lot easier than Cassius Clay who said "I don't mind beating up people, but I don't believe in killing nobody," and whose refusal to be drafted landed him in jail and stripped him of his heavyweight boxing title.

I received my draft notice and was told to report to a center in Brooklyn on the date that my wife was expecting our first child. I applied for a delay on those grounds while I pondered the remaining options before me. One was to go to Canada. The other, since I was eligible only for the Doctor's draft (being in my thirties, too old to become a grunt), was to refuse the commission that physicians were given, for doctors in the armed forces start out as officers. Thus, I would be a doctor/private and I felt sure this would cause them problems. For starters, my having to salute everyone who came to see me while nobody would have to initiate a salute to me was bound to grind down a few gears of this military machine: not a good thing in a rigorously rigid chain-of-command system. Fortunately for me, this delay was granted, and in the next call-up of doctors, they were taking younger physicians, unfortunately for them.

But I was really pissed off. If Lyndon Johnson wanted my ass, I wanted his. So the next phase of my anti-war activities was to start the first "Dump-Johnson" group, *Citizens for Kennedy/Fulbright*, aimed at drafting an anti-war ticket of Senators Robert Kennedy and Bill Fulbright. Former congressman Charles Porter, another "peace" democrat from Oregon, and myself served as co-chairmen. We organized chapters in most states and had a slate of delegates pledged to Kennedy, headed by another maverick, Eugene Daniel, ready for the New Hampshire primary. These successes helped pave the way for Eugene McCarthy to challenge LBJ and we felt both elated and fulfilled when Johnson decided not to run. With Johnson's withdrawal, Robert Kennedy entered the race only to be assassinated, and we were left with Hubert Humphrey, who was Johnson's vice-president, or Richard Nixon. It was akin to sailing between Scylla and Charybdus. And so the war went on for five more years.

When the Iraqi invasion seemed imminent, I took stock, thought that I had too few years left—or energy for—that sort of protest again. Still, I felt I had to do something. That something consisted of sending money to organizations like *Move On* and *True Majority* that opposed the Iraqi war, signing their email petitions, contributing to the candidacy of Howard Dean, and writing press releases for his local supporters. Then it occurred to me to take a different approach to protest; a musical approach, for there was no protest music to be heard on the airways. When Natalie Maines, the lead singer of The Dixie Chicks said she was ashamed of being a Texan due to George Bush's Iraqi policies, the right-wing Fundamentalists were outraged and the group was banned from their Clear Channel radio station airplays. Nor were any stars rushing in to fill the void: Madonna? Michael Jackson? Rappers? Bruce Springsteen? This new breed of performing artists were not like the Arlo Guthries, Pete Seegers, the Beatles, or other musicians who professed opposition to the war in Vietnam, and they did not seem inclined to take financial risks or have their careers suffer by opposing Bush's rush toward unilateral invasion.

Fortunately, my compadres and I were freer. As Kris Kristofferson wrote in his song, *Me and Bobby McGee*, "Freedom's just another word for nothing left to lose," and being musical nobodies we had nothing to lose. And so *Mumbo Jumbo* was recorded and launched. We even took out an Internet website in an attempt to give the song away: *www.thecompatriots.com*.

Resenting George Bush's definition of "patriotism" we called ourselves "The Compatriots." The "we" consisted of Andrew Baker, owner of Harbor Music Studios in Sag Harbor and some of his staff (Brett Warren, who taught guitar, and Carolina Giraldo, a high school student who worked at the studio part time), myself and two others I worked with at *The Permanent Press* (Elise D'Haene, a novelist, screenwriter, former psychotherapist, out-front lesbian, good singer, and our Associate Publisher, and her sister, Maureen D'Haene, an out-front heterosexual, personal trainer, mother of two, and now our Managing Editor), and Armand LaMacchia, once a studio drummer and school teacher, still a great cook and currently a restaurant owner and psychotherapist .

Despite our efforts we only had two airway plays that I know of: Harry Minot, station director of WPKN, the FM Station of the University of Bridgeport, played it, as did a station in Byron Bay, Australia. We approached all of the Pacifica stations and each of their music directors. Each promised to get back to us, but none of them did. This was another great irony since Pacifica was launched by pacifists. A.J. Muste and Dave Dellinger, avowed pacifists, organized the first opposition to the Vietnam War. But, as Dylan said, "The times they are a'changin'." Nonetheless it was a noble effort and we received a lot of hits on our web site. And if you are reading this, Madonna or Bruce, I give you full recording rights for free.

***Mumbo Jumbo** was recorded at Harbor Music Studio in Sag Harbor in March, 2003, with Andrew Baker playing bass and tambourine, Armand LaMacchia on drums, Joel Brett Warren on guitar; Maureen D'Haene on tambourine and in the chorus, Carolina Giraldo sang in the chorus, Elise D'Haene sang solo and chorus, and I played soprano and alto saxophones and sang alternate lines with Elise.*

# CONVERSATION

***Conversation*** was recorded in Virgin Gorda in February 2004. I played alto saxophone and Marcus Mark played all other instruments.

## CONVERSATION

After writing a couple of songs with lyrics, I wanted to take a break and do something with melody alone. Over the course of a few weeks I kept making false starts, jotting down some phrase that would occur quite by accident, but went no further. Then I thought, "Why not string all of these together as a song?" My plan was to repeat each phrase before moving on—to make it seem both purposeful and more musical. I envisioned playing it as a call and response: I'd play the first phrase and John Okas, a fellow saxophonist, would respond. John's a friend, neighbor, and an author of ours (*Routes* and *The Freewayfarers Book of the Dead*, two social satires, filled with puns and word play, as well as two wonderful cookbooks: *Sicilian American Pasta* and *Sicilian American Cooking*). He also has a small studio in his house where we could play. Elise, after hearing the tune, suggested that I title it *Conversation*, and so I did. It seemed even more apt because John, aside from being a much more accomplished horn player than I am, is one of the most entertaining conversationalists I know. Looking like a younger and handsomer version of the comic David Brenner, he has the unique ability to turn concepts on their heads, offering opinions that go against the conventional grain, yet have a logic all their own that one might never have considered before. Outrageous at times, funny at others, both playful and serious, he's a treat to be around for he always makes you think.

And so it came to pass that, in January 2004, we

scheduled a few hours each week at his house to work on the song and after several weeks we had a rough cut. For me, though, something wasn't right. Perhaps it was all the prerecorded drumbeats, or the addition of other sounds he added by playing the keyboard. Whatever it was, it seemed both mechanical and somewhat muddled. Then came a break, as Judy and I headed off for our annual February vacation in Virgin Gorda, with plans to record another song with Marcus, *Serendipity*, for which I wanted an "Island feel." While I was down there, it occurred to me that Marcus was the best musician that I knew, so why not try him with *Conversation* and two other songs and see what he would do with all four of them.

What he did worked far better, though it also minimized the back and forth, call/recall, that I originally intended. I thought it might work as a musical introduction to this chapter, where I might touch on a hodgepodge of things I felt strongly about, bits and pieces of this and that. Given the original structuring of the tune, might it not be better to rename it *Bits and Pieces*? Still, what's in a name? Whether you call your dog Rover or Argus, it's still the same dog. Intentions count, as do sounds, and *Conversation* has a more pleasing sound for a song than *Bits & Pieces*. And it does allow me to write this chapter as a conversation—a conversation with myself, using a question and answer format with, hopefully, a small measure of John Okas' provocativeness.

**Question:** What do you mean by that?
**Answer:** A decade ago, in a dinner table conversation with friends, there was talk of who should be appointed to fill a vacancy on the Supreme Court. Several leading candidates names were tossed about. When it came my turn to

speak, I proposed Judge Wopner, the original judge of *The People's Court* back in the 1980s.

**Question:** A judge from a television show? That's so superficial. You can't be serious.

**Answer:** I'm perfectly serious. We pay homage to the chief justices and presume they have the integrity and wisdom to interpret the law properly and fairly. But really, when it comes right down to it, there is rarely any agreement on the law. If you doubt that, how do you explain so many split decisions recorded by this great deliberative body? Judges are nominated by Presidents, who invariably seek to advance their own political agendas, and are then submitted to Congress for confirmation. This is hardly a recipe for detached objectivity.

But Judge Wopner seemed different. He had no political agenda. His popularity was based upon the fact that he weighed issues carefully, listened well, always appeared fair minded, had the intelligence to render verdicts that made perfect sense, and never show-boated the way that later reality show judges like Judge Judy or Ed Koch did.

Who would you rather have sitting on a case, Judge Wopner, Antonin Scalia, or Clarence Thomas?

**Question:** What is it you want to cover in this chapter?
**Answer:** Bits and pieces. Anything that comes up in this conversation. Things I've thought about and things in which I have first hand experiences. Health. Medicine. Elaborations on themes I've introduced earlier. My observations about the body politic; about society, how it functions and perpetuates itself; on resistance to change; shortcomings in the way we educate people; and "human stupidity," if you'll allow me to use that politically incorrect term.

**Question:** What makes you think anybody would be interested in your opinions?

**Answer:** That's a good question. My wife raised it, as any publisher might, when I told her I was starting this book. "Why should anyone want to read what you have to say? You're not a celebrity, so what makes you think you can sell many copies?" She is certainly correct on that count. Were I to change my name to Donald Trump or Al Gore, Johnny Depp or Barbara Bush, I'm certain I'd have a built-in audience. But as I told Judy, "What's the big deal? We've published a lot of good books by a lot of good writers and usually sell between 500 and 2,500 copies after all the returns are in. So having a large audience isn't that critical. Besides, it's a challenging project and there are a lot of things I'd like to get off my chest."

**Question:** Including further comments on the subject of the law?

**Answer**: Yes. *Too many laws, too many lawyers!* We have a Congress whose sole purpose seems to be drafting more laws, amendments to laws, exceptions to laws, and loopholes to tax law that are broad enough to drive a hundred Brink's trucks through, side-by-side, carrying a gazillion dollars back into the accounts of their corporate friends and the special interests that finance Congressmen's campaigns. What hypocrisy!

**Question:** In what sense?

**Answer:** In the sense that there is a two-tiered society being created here: where the legislators are not subject to the same demands and standards that they impose upon others.

**Question:** Can you give some other examples?

**Answer:** Easily. Just pick up the paper and you can see the contradictions. The other day I read about an investigation into the use of drugs in professional sports in which Congressmen are pushing for greater drug testing of athletes, just as state and local lawmakers have demanded drug testing in schools and for applicants to certain jobs. Well what's good for the goose should be good for the gander, don't you think? Why should legislators be immune from the same random drug testing that they require of others? This is one glaring example of hypocrisy. Test yourselves first, I would preach, before you start testing others.

And while we are at it, why do non-governmental wage earners, like myself, have to pay taxes that cover health and retirement benefits for government workers when the taxes of government workers don't pay for our health and retirement benefits?

Lincoln's Gettysburg address promised us an enduring "government of, by, and for the people." Why is it, then, that the salaries and perks of congressmen so far exceed the salaries of the average person? A government "of the people" would seem to require this equity of income, lest we turn into a government "of the elite, by the elite, and for the elite"—which is, sadly, the case.

**Question:** You are very critical about law and lawyers.

**Answer:** Truthfully, I have some close friends who are both lawyers and good people, and I respect what they do. It just seems that too often laws and lawyers are part of society's problems, and not the solution. That's why they are the butt of so many jokes.

**Question:** Do you have a favorite?

**Answer:** I do. Two lawyers are sitting on the beach when an exquisitely beautiful young woman wearing a bikini walks by. As she passes, one lawyer says to the other, "Boy, would I like to fuck her." "Out of what?" the other answers.

**Question:** You've also spent a lot of time and words criticizing America. How come? Do you see no merit here?

**Answer:** The one indisputable beauty of today's America and, perhaps, its greatest accomplishment, is that it is so ethnically heterogeneous. Hispanics, Asians, Blacks, and Whites are everywhere. Every major religious group—along with us unaffiliated types—are scattered alongside one another in every state of the union. Because of that the sort of tribal warfare that has appeared in so many places around the world is inconceivable here. That is no small blessing.

I'm critical of America because I *love* living here and would like to see us have a more compassionate and enlightened governance. I also believe that citizens of every country in the world have, as a first obligation, to be a critic of their own government rather than a critic of someone else's. Let's not point fingers at China or Russia or France or Cuba as a way of diverting attention from our own shortcomings.

When I was a practicing psychotherapist it was axiomatic that the faults we see in others are, more often than not, the very same things that we hide from ourselves. Political leadership translates this somewhat differently: the faults they point out in others are an excellent way of diverting the public's attention from those same faults that they practice.

Mort Sahl, the social critic who revolutionized stand-up comedy from the 1950s onward used to walk on stage, read from and comment on the stories in the daily newspaper. Here's how he described his own brand of humor: "Will Rogers used to come out with a newspaper and pretend he was a yokel criticizing the intellectuals who ran the government. I come out with a newspaper and pretend I'm an intellectual making fun of the yokels running the government."

I write this section after reading *The New York Times* this morning (March 15, 2004), which would have provided plenty of grist for Sahl's sardonic wit. On page three, there was this announcement: ***As Expected, Putin Wins a Second Term in Russia***, with the subheading reading ***On Election Day, the U.S. Scolds Moscow on Democracy***. President Bush's National Security Advisor, Condeleeza Rice, criticized limitations on opposition campaigning, others spoke of "overbearing government manipulation," and Secretary of State Colin Powell was quoted as saying that "Russians have to understand that to have full democracy of the kind that the international community will recognize, you've got to let candidates have the same access to the media that the president had," and he urged Mr. Putin to "do a better job in making democracy work."

Now let's look at the story on page one: "Federal investigators are scrutinizing television segments in which the Bush administration paid people to pose as journalists praising the new Medicare law, which would help elderly Americans with the costs of their prescription medications. The videos are intended for use in local television news shows. Several included pictures of President Bush receiving a standing ovation from a cheering crowd as he signed the Medicare law on Dec. 8." It turns out these videos shown on local news programs were made by his Department of Human Services, and that "the government also prepared scripts to be read by news anchors introducing what the administration describes as a made-for-television 'story package'."

Tell me how this differs from the manipulations our government accuses the Russians of? In our 2000 presidential election, George Bush outspent Al Gore, his Democratic challenger, by a two-to-one margin by virtue of his corporate fund-raising abilities, thus dominating television advertising. And let us not forget that George Bush became President despite losing the popular vote, including the votes in Florida when, after the election, those state-wide votes were recounted. He was put into office by the Supreme Court (where was Judge Wopner when we needed him?). Might not Colin Powell just as aptly say to America and his own administration that "*we* have to do a better job in making *our* democracy work?"

We call for democracies abroad, yet routinely destroy these democracies, replacing them with dictators when democratic leadership defies our corporate goals. Fifty years ago we deposed Premier Mohammed Mossadegh, and replaced him with Shah Reza Pahlavi. Mossadegh, *Time* magazine's "Man of the Year in 1951," was freely elected, but he was threatening to end foreign control of Iran's oil fields and so, in 1953, the CIA arranged a coup and installed the authoritarian Shah who ran Iran as an American client state for a quarter century. But the 1979 revolution led to the ascension of the Muslim fundamentalist government of Ayatollah Koumeni, so that we are now paying a great price for this initial interference. In 1973, the CIA plotted a similar coup against another democrat, Salvadore Allende of Chile, the head of another left-leaning democratic government that was perceived as threatening American interests. So the CIA went to work again, replacing Allende with another despot, General Augusto Pinochet, who did his best to rid Chile of leftist opposition by executing thousands of his fellow-countrymen.

For all of our posturing about being the guiding light for democracies around the world and the betterment of man, our deeds don't match our words except when it's convenient. Nor do we have the best democracy or the most compassionate social system. We do, though, have the largest prison population per capita in the world and, after an inmate has served his debt to society, he is forever deprived of his democratic right to vote. Many other governments are far more advanced on these counts than we are. Smaller westernized countries, both population-wise and geographic-wise (Denmark, Norway, Sweden, the Netherlands, Iceland, and New Zealand quickly come to mind), do better than us because citizens have closer personal contact with their elected officials and can more readily spot scoundrels. These states also have more advanced educational systems, better social contracts and safety nets for their populace, and less of a gap between the very rich and very poor. In America that gap keeps growing. Nearly every industrialized country has universal health coverage. Yet we, the richest nation on earth, are told we can't afford it.

**Question:** Why do you think Americans tolerate these situations?

**Answer:** Generally speaking, I attribute it to stupidity, but this is not unique to America. It's in the human genetic code. It's endemic around the world. Ariel Sharon assumed the premiership in Israel after promising that his tougher stance toward the Palestinians would bring security. In fact, the level of violence and counter violence increased ten-fold. When the next election was held, poll numbers showed that 80% of Israelis were in favor of removing settlements in the West Bank and Gaza and in favor of trading land for peace. Yet Sharon's party, Likud, defeated Labor, whose positions accurately reflected public sentiment. This can only be attributed to an incomprehensible level of stupidity, though I realize one could make it sound kinder by saying that Israelis were "misled" or "manipulated." But I will stick with "stupid." And Americans are no different.

Public relations people and advertisers never underestimate the degree of stupidity in society. Watch all the vacuous phrases—referred to as "sound bites" by the "handlers" in political campaigns—or the claims made in product promotion. The fact that so many citizens swallow these pitches and are influenced by them is brought about, initially, by an educational system that fails to teach children to think independently, to read between the lines, and to identify the ways they are manipulated. "The child is the father of the man" it's been said, and if the child is not taught to look behind the veil of authority, or is not taught to "think outside the box," the man will be as underdeveloped as the child, and just as blindly play follow-the-leader. Herman Goering, one of the Nazi leaders, testifying at his war crimes trail in Nuremberg put this truth bluntly:

> "Of course the people don't want war. But after all, it's the leaders of the country who determine the policy, and it's always a simple matter to drag the people along whether it's a democra-

cy, a fascist dictatorship, or a parliament, or a communist dictatorship. Voice or no voice, the people can always be brought to the bidding of the leaders. That is easy. All you have to do is tell them they are being attacked, and denounce the pacifists for lack of patriotism, and exposing the country to greater danger."

Doesn't this sound familiar?

**Question:** Are you referring to the way we were led into the war in Iraq?

**Answer:** I'm referring to the way we are led into so many of our wars. Take Vietnam. We were told that the North Vietnamese were a threat to our security, that a ship was attacked in the Tonkin Gulf, and if Vietnam were reunited under communist rule, the "Domino" effect would produce ripples that would place us in danger. Well, after a long bloody struggle and tens of thousands of deaths on both sides, we lost that war. Vietnam was united under the communists, no other regime toppled in Southeast Asia, and America was not invaded. We did the same thing with Mexico in years past, and with Spain in Teddy Roosevelt's time, when we fought the "enemy" in Cuba. We invaded Panama to get rid of the "threat" posed by the dangerous General Manual Noriega for being involved in the drug trade. This was part of our "War on Drugs," we were told, and had nothing to do with Noriega's interest in reclaiming Panamanian sovereignty over the Panama Canal. So being manipulated into war with Iraq is nothing new. Give Herman Goering credit, even if he was a Nazi, for telling the truth. Leaders can always get us to go to war. And they love declaring other wars as well.

**Question:** How so?

**Answer:** How so? The War on Drugs has been going on since I was born and I'm 70 years old. Another 30 years and it will have been going on for nearly as long as the Hundred Years War between the British and the French, a series of battles that began in 1337 and ended in 1453. And guess what? Drug usage has been growing each and every year that this war has been fought. Is it not time to make "Peace with Drugs," just as we made peace with the Vietnamese when that war proved unwinnable? Just look at how other countries handle this. The Netherlands has not made any War on Drugs, and yet it has not become a nation of addicts. In our War on Drugs you can buy cocaine, marijuana, ecstasy, steroids, heroin, or hallucinogens on street corners and in schools throughout America. Except the prices are a lot higher than they are in countries that have not banned them. Our prisons are filled with many non-violent people who were simply making a living selling drugs, as well as addicts who would steal to afford them.

The idiocy of the War on Drugs was especially painful to me, for I lost my youngest son, Yan, to a heroin overdose. The "War" did not prevent him from buying marijuana, cocaine, and heroin while he was attending high school, nor did it offer immediate treatment facilities at those times when he seemed ready to do tentative battle with his descent into addiction. Instead, he would have to apply for and wait weeks for "openings," by which time he was off and running again. Why no funds? The expenditures for this war are so heavily weighted in favor of police actions, interdictions, border guards, costly incarceration, the need for more prisons, and overseas actions, including defoliating suspected growing areas in Latin

America, that little is left to provide accessible treatment facilities.

It's increasingly apparent that our government won't change its approach for two reasons: the first being that right-wing Moralists, abetted by the politicians that toady to them, think that a kindlier and more compassionate approach would, again, be rewarding "Vice and Immorality." The other reason is that there is a virtual army in place carrying out this war; an army that will fight for its share of taxpayer money despite waging a losing battle. Of course, our government did launch, with great fanfare, Nancy Reagan's sloganeering "Just Say No" campaign, though only the dumbest of the dumb would believe that this has saved anyone.

One would think we would have learned better by looking at what happened when another group of Moralists passed a Constitutional Amendment banning liquor, which they felt was having destructive social effects. Anyone caught buying, selling, smuggling, or manufacturing beer or alcohol faced serious prison time. What happened? An underground economy, much like today's underground drug economy, replaced above-board sales. Here, too, the game of "cops and robbers" proved ineffective. Illegal stills, alcohol smuggled in from overseas, speakeasies that provided what customers wanted, and bribes to law enforcement officials enabled a river of booze to keep flowing. Eventually, prohibition was seen as the failure it was, and the Amendment that established it was repealed. Once repealed, did we turn into a nation of drunkards? Of course not. Nor would we turn into a nation of drug addicts if drugs were made legal, simply because most people realize that being drunk constantly or high constantly is not the way they want to live life.

Another irony—and example of hypocrisy—concerning our War on Drugs is this: after deposing Noriega, we not only allowed, but actually helped, the Nicaraguan Contras deal drugs. The profits from these lucrative sales were used to pay for the weapons that U.S. Lieutenant Colonel Oliver North illegally supplied to support their war against the Sandanistas. North, who was never indicted for lying to Congress about his illegal arms dealing, was considered another "patriot" by the right-wing in this country, for trying to save us from another "grave threat:" a third world country whose leftist policies were perceived as a serious menace, for if they succeeded other poor Central American countries might attempt to end exploitative U.S. policies. They were selling the Domino theory all over again.

**Question:** You've talked a lot about the war in Iraq, and most of what you've said has been negative. Do you see no good at all in it?
**Answer:** Well, we did get rid of Saddam Hussein, a very cruel and ruthless man, though on balance it does not seem worth it when over 12,000 Americans were killed or wounded by December 2004, as well as more than one hundred thousand Iraqi's killed and tens of thousands wounded, the great majority being non-combatant casualties stemming from our very own weapons of mass destruction: our bombs, rockets, and overwhelming firepower. Of course, we don't hear many reports on Iraqi casualties for they are the "other," and we don't value their lives as much as the lives of our own tribe. But there is one very positive aspect of this war.

**Question:** Which is what?

**Answer:** That it will likely mark the beginning-of-the-end of the Anglo-American Empire. The Brits have always bragged that the "sun never set" on their empire, and even today vestiges remain around the world in the form of the British Commonwealth. In the mid 1900s the baton was passed to its former colony, America. But the George Bush/Tony Blair alliance that unilaterally swept us into Iraq has drawn public opposition in every country on earth save for Israel. Much of Europe is united as never before, with its common currency, the Euro, replacing the dollar in value and the European Union tying these nations together through the European Parliament. There is increasing sentiment to form a European Defense Force separate from NATO and the American military. Going it alone has stretched us too thin, and the bill for occupying Iraq will cost us billions of dollars for years to come.

Even before the Iraqi invasion America spent more money on its military *than the rest of the world combined*! With the vastly increased expenditures necessary to pay for our occupation and "nation building" in Iraq, as well as keeping our armies in Afghanistan, we are about to collapse under these debts. Our balance of payments and deficits are looking more like those of a third world country and this is an unsustainable situation, Alan Greenspan's opinions to the contrary. No wonder we can't afford universal health care for our citizens when our greatest expenditures go for policing the world.

So I look forward to our becoming a lesser power. The Dutch, the Swiss, and the Japanese have shown how well people can do when they mind their own business, don't have any substantial defense budgets, and have no interest in taking on the world. So have the Scandinavian countries. Let us become one of them and spend our tax dollars to improve the lot of our own citizens.

**Question:** Anything else you'd care to add here?
**Answer:** Yes. The public is constantly being manipulated by playing to fear, and death is the ultimate fear. Besides mobilizing a populace to keep large armies for fear of being exterminated by some outside enemy, it's also used to sell insurance, to drive people into doctors' offices for unnecessary treatments, and for all sorts of unnecessary testing. A physician friend of mine has told me that over 80% of patients coming to see him have nothing wrong with them. It's reassurance they want. That's what brings them in. Unawareness of the relationship between lifestyle, exercise, and food intake, along with a willingness to cede responsibility for one's health to the "expert," leads to a passivity that encourages the very illnesses people fear.

The greatest scare tactics are provided by local television news broadcast: "A mother and her children killed by a hit and run in Duluth... A landslide in Mount Blanc takes five lives... A fire in Milwaukee kills two children... An infant left in a dumpster in Cleveland... A sniper kills four in Washington..." and on and on and on. It's really *old news*, recycled again and again, with new people and events that fit the same format, sustaining and deepening our worst fears and concerns. I can hear the producers now: "Let's make people worry until we cut to the next commercial," which are often for pharmaceuticals you can "ask your doctor about" in case you're worried about high blood pressure, strokes, heart attacks, cancer, or have erectile problems. And you *should* be worried about these conditions, for all these illnesses are featured on "in depth coverage" on these same programs.

It's laughable to see telecasts reporting on periodic congressional hearings looking for links between violence in our communities and the media. The culprits routinely trotted out are violent Hollywood movies and rap singers, when the chief offenders are sitting right under our noses: the news shows, supposedly doing objective reporting, but always favoring violent events.

**Question:** What is your take on medicine as it's practiced today?

**Answer:** It's very difficult for both physicians and patients, as everyone is looking over the physician's shoulder. Perfection is expected and, under fear of lawsuits, patients are subjected to many unnecessary tests in order to ensure that the chart will look right if a lawsuit is brought. And because there are so many lawsuits, malpractice insurance is so astronomically high that these costs are not only passed on to the patient, but have led to the premature retirement of many older doctors and dentists who had cut down to a part-time practice, but couldn't make ends meet because of the full time malpractice insurance policies they needed. And the paperwork! I have physician friends who don't bother to bill Medicare, Medicaid, or insurance companies for certain procedures and care-giving because the billing processes and forms to fill out cost more in secretarial help than the payments they receive. What other profession has to endure so many lawsuits despite the practitioner doing his best? Can you imagine auto mechanics being sued in such proportions when they fail to fix a car?

Another big problem is the assumption that early diagnostics are necessary to prevent serious consequences later on. Thus, the populace has always been encouraged to have yearly check-ups. Being a doctor, I've never bought into this concept and, increasingly, other physicians at leading teaching hospitals are now, in growing numbers, saying the same thing. One was quoted in a *New York Times* article a year or so ago giving his definition of a healthy person: "One who hasn't had a thorough workup." And once anything is found that is "questionable," be it in a blood test or X-ray or physical examination, there follows a commitment to more tests and treatments, all of which increase a person's level of anxiety and "dis-ease"—which encourages "disease."

This is very apparent in the approach to prostate cancer, the illusion being that "if we catch it early we can cure it." Thus the push for early screening. There are routine PSA tests which, if elevated, lead to biopsies which, if evidence of cancer is found, lead to surgery, radiation, chemotherapy or a combination of these three treatments. However, when you consider that the vast majority of men who come to autopsy after the age of 55 show histological evidence of prostate cancer even though they died of something else (the rates approaches 80% when men are in their 60s and older), the only conclusion to be drawn is that prostate cancer is not so much a disease as it is a part of the normal aging process. Studies in Europe have shown that men who are not treated for prostate cancer have a better survival rate than those who are. Little wonder, since radiation can also cause cancer and biopsies can spread them. Add that to the fact that chemotherapy also destroys the body's immune reaction and you have a pretty primitive system of treatment here.

Six years ago I woke up in the middle of the night unable to void. Judy drove me to Southampton Hospital where I was catheterized. It's a most painful procedure. I agreed to a PSA test but knew I would refuse treatment, work-ups, or further testing no matter what it showed, since there are so many false positives and false negatives (mine did come back negative). Before being released I was prescribed one of the standard drugs to relax the muscles at the base of the bladder so as to minimize future blocking, advised to take another pharmaceutical that is supposed to shrink enlarged prostates, and told it would be necessary to take these medications indefinitely until that time when I would surely require surgery.

For the first week, every time I peed there was a burning pain resulting from the abrasion caused by the catheter, and I took the medications faithfully in order to avoid a second trip back to the hospital. But as soon as the burning ended I stopped taking these pills for two reasons: the first being that they caused impotency. When a guy gets up in years, the penis is slower to rise and quicker to fall. (Talking to an unmarried friend and neighbor one day I asked him if he practiced safe sex. "Very difficult," he answered. "You get aroused to start with, but interrupting and trying to slip on a condom is like trying to put an oyster in a slot machine.") I was certainly not about to give up my sex life, because that's not the kind of living I envisioned, and taking away this great pleasure would lessen life's quality significantly.

Speaking to friends and reading the literature it was also clear that there were good natural alternatives that few physicians in the U.S. were prescribing, but that were used readily in Europe and also available here in health food stores; these were saw palmetto and pygeum, which I have taken regularly. I also radically changed parts of my diet: no caffeine and no liquor, prostate irritants that are easy to give up once you've had the experience of catheterization. I've taken fewer than four-dozen bladder-relaxing pills in the past six years, using them on nights I was having difficulty voiding. I've also sat in numerous sitz baths if the flow is not coming. And I'm still around, still able to fuck, and glad for my decision. Had I not been a skeptical physician and not seen friends die of prostate cancer after "early diagnosis and treatment," I'm sure I would have bought into the approved medical advice I was given.

The insistence that "testing is essential" applies to women as well. Mammograms, once routine, have since proved themselves to be unreliable and largely unnecessary without accompanying symptoms. I believe that the same case can be made for pap smears. Neither Judy nor I go for regular check-ups. If there is a persisting symptom that doesn't clear up within a few weeks, we're not averse to consultations. But one can only live once and you have to decide whether you want to live in fear of death or savor life. Running off to see a doctor in the hope that if you catch something early enough you will live forever is folly. No one dies of "natural causes" or old age anymore. It's always from a disease—cancer, heart disease, strokes. Ultimately, I believe that all these so-called illnesses are nature's way of saying bye-bye, for life must lead to death from the moment of birth, and it shall ever be so.

Personally, I've come to believe that, in a profound and mysterious way, death is an illusion, and represents nothing more and nothing less than a morphing of one consciousness into another, since all matter has its own consciousness. Does a butterfly remember its former life as a caterpillar? I think not. The caterpillar dies, but the butterfly emerges from this death. It's not an ending as much as it is a transformation, a passing on to another form. I won't press this argument here, for I've already made it in my book *Dying*, which was written to help people overcome their own fears about death as well as enabling them to be of greater assistance to those undergoing this transition.

Yet this life is a great gift and worth sustaining. It's been said before by many others, but it's worth saying again: one of the best ways to maintain health is to pay attention to the dictum "You are what you eat." So many people eat unhealthy foods: fast foods, fatty foods, foods with additives and preservatives which prolong shelf life or produce a more attractive and palatable color. This is not helpful, however, for prolonging human life. Witness Bill Clinton, known for his overindulgence on these foods, needing heart bypass surgery at a comparatively young age. One simple rule in shopping is to read labels in supermarkets and reject any foodstuff that has chemicals or additives in it, and to purchase organic foods and unprocessed foods whenever possible. It may be more expensive to buy organic foods, but you might save substantially on your medical bills. Regular exercise is another very important ingredient for wellness and longevity, but so many people are just too lazy. They eat poorly, do not exercise, and rely on check-ups with their doctor, hoping to hear that there's nothing wrong with them. Then they can postpone changing an unhealthy life style, and hope that they will be given a pill to clear up any damage they've already done to themselves.

**Question:** Would you describe yourself as a pessimist? Do you see no solutions for some of these problems?

**Answer:** I wouldn't call myself a pessimist, but a realist. Solutions are easy, conceptually, but very hard to bring about. Society is in a constant equilibrium, so that if you try to address one problem, an opposition is always called forth, maintaining the status quo. Take education, for example.

Many years ago I worked in the school system and saw two gaping holes in how we educate youngsters, one being that we don't teach self-awareness and psychology early enough. It should take place starting from the very first classes, just as the three R's are taught. What good does it do to learn reading skills, writing skills and arithmetic if you don't learn interactive social skills? Enter any classroom and you'll find disruptive children. Go into the schoolyard and the bullies will appear. Watch what happens when some students are unmercifully teased, ridiculed, or shunned. It's par for the course in growing up, yet nobody addresses the fears, hurt feelings, or feelings of inadequacy that arise. Nor do the bullies and cut-ups ever learn how their peers see them. Here's a simple solution: a period devoted to encouraging discussion of these issues in a circular group setting, facilitated by a teacher trained to bring these hidden, unspoken feelings to the forefront. "How did you feel, Mary, when Sally made fun of you this morning? Who is the scariest person in this class, kids? Let's go around the room and everybody name someone. And if you're afraid to name a person, maybe we'll write it all out in secret ballots, see what the vote is and what this means to the winner and to the rest of you… Are you surprised that you were selected Johnny?… How would you like your classmates to treat you, Sam?" Before you knew it you'd have awareness training and feedback that can only be helpful and illuminating, and lead to other interpersonal discussions.

I volunteered to give a course like this when, in my thirties, I worked as a consulting psychiatrist to the New York City Board of Education and again, as a private citizen, when I moved to Nyack, New York, in my forties. But guess what? It was impossible to provide this service, even for free. Why? Too much opposition from parents who were afraid that their children might start to talk about their home lives, or be "brainwashed," and from teachers who feared it would impinge upon or threaten their curriculum.

The other shortcoming is that no elementary or high school I know of offers comprehensive courses in human health and disease that teach how the body functions, the ways to tell the differences between viral and bacterial infections, how the heart, lungs, liver, and kidneys work, and how various foodstuffs and drugs affect us. Knowledge about these things should not be reserved for medical students and biology majors. Learning what medical students learn in graduate school, but on a simplified level, starting at an early age, would be a great boon. If children were taught this early on, they'd be better able to recognize problems and participate in health decisions in later life. Yet here, too, there were no takers when I volunteered such a program. Can't tell you why, exactly, but it seemed somehow threatening to the administrators running the schools, maybe simply because it hadn't been done before.

Here's another example of how simple remedies are hard to apply. Having also worked at a prison, Rikers Island in New York in my late thirties, I can attest that once jailed, the inmate has no real responsibilities. All important decisions are made for him. Food is provided, conflicts are decided by the authorities, and there is no attempt to teach responsibility or have them participate in their own governance. Surprising, because one thing that the majority of inmates suffer from involves not taking responsibility. Leaving all this responsibility in the hands of others requires a lot of staffing and costs a great deal of money. I did some research and discovered it would be far cheaper to house prisoners on a cruise ship, offshore, thus protecting society, than it was to keep them in jail. I wrote a piece for *The Village Voice* at the time, making these arguments. If inmates had to plan their own menus and, in a land-based prison system, grow their own food, or had an opportunity to take more responsibility for their own care, important lessons could be learned. I spelled out ways it might be structured and initiated. Such reforms would necessarily affect the traditional habits and jobs of the prisoners' custodians. Resistance to the idea of giving up any of their control understandably rose, once again and proposals to change fell on deafened ears.

Such is the way of life everywhere. Settled societies have a great built-in resistance to change. And one has to accept this.

**Question:** How about a sum up? This conversation has gone on long enough. See if you can keep it short.

**Answer:** Okay.

When young, we are ready to do battle. With age comes the realization that acceptance of the ways of the world is also a necessity. If social change is to come about it starts with changes in our individual lives.

There are no permanent solutions to the problems of the world, for the human genetic code doesn't seem to allow for it. Those who preach love—the Christs, the Ghandis, the Martin Luther Kings—give rise to great movements in times that are ripe for change and when people are tired of conflict, social injustice, and domination. But these gentler souls threaten the established order and are often martyred for their decency. When they fall, their followers tend to reestablish the same structures that the flag-bearer fought and, given the warts in all of us—avarice, power, domination, exploitation—conflict returns.

So embrace your own contradictions. Don't be part of the herd. Don't be afraid to question authority. Tend your own garden well, do it with love and caring, and set an example for others through your own behavior. It's better than debating with, bullying, or trying to reform your neighbor for his shortcomings.

*SERENDIPITY*

## SERENDIPITY

If you are one who thinks that you are master of your fate
That charm and your intelligence have brought a perfect mate
You might recall that pride will often come before a fall
So I hope you will consider that you haven't done it all.

You never got to choose the circumstances of your birth
The country you were born in, your parents or their worth
Your sex or inclinations and your strengths and weakness too
Are not things to take credit for, but programmed into you.

Serendipity, my friend. Hopefully you'll see
That much of who you are results from serendipity.
Serendipity, my friend. It's obvious to me
That much of who we are results from serendipity.

When one examines past events without a point-of-view
It's clear that many chance encounters made the current you.
Ambition and hard work deserve a very special place
Still strangers, friends, and lovers helped to form your present base.

The world needs fewer egotists who act so self-assured.
Their arrogance is like a sickness begging to be cured.
Zealots, moralizers, politicians, CEOs
Could use a dose of humbleness if mankind is to grow.

Serendipity, my friends. I pray that they will see
That all their acquisitions stem from serendipity.
Serendipity, my friend, it gives us gifts for free.
One's opportunities all stem from serendipity.

The whys and wherefores of our lives are one big mystery.
Some call it God, some call it Fate, some call it Destiny.
These powerful conceptions should inspire humility
As each one manifests itself as serendipity.

Serendipity, my friend. It's very clear to me
That what we have become results from serendipity.
Serendipity, my friend I hold it dear to me
And pray that lessened egos lead to worldwide harmony.

## SERENDIPITY

Seventeen years ago, in 1987, I found myself walking our property, a 22-acre parcel that we had purchased five years earlier for a song. It was an exquisite spring day, and the foliage was brilliantly green. I had just passed our book warehouse, walked by my studio and headed for the pond, where dragonflies hovered and a pair of Canada geese and three of their goslings were swimming, frogs were croaking, birds were calling, and we had just paid off the mortgage.

I reached my arms out in a heavenly embrace, looked at the sky, and surprised myself by saying "Thank you Lord. I did nothing to deserve this." That I did nothing to deserve this is, I believe, true. The surprise came from giving thanks to the "Lord," for I am not a believer in an anthropomorphic God or the Heaven he supposedly inhabits. Yet, I have repeated this "Thank you" often since then.

I might just as well have said "Thank you Destiny," or "Thank you Fate," two conceptions that equally accept the notion that forces beyond human contemplation and understanding bring either blessings or hardship to our lives. Once you accept this truism, you must also accept that we don't necessarily get what we think we deserve in life. Particularly when, in looking about, you find scoundrels who are rewarded with riches and fame, and decent hardworking folk who are mired in poverty and anonymity.

One of our cultural assumptions is that, by virtue of planning, education, and putting your nose to the grindstone, you will reap a success for which you can take credit. This concept, taught in both subtle and not-so-subtle ways through books, stories, film, and schools has lead to an excessive number of egomaniacs: folks who presume that an elevated worldly position is a result of their brilliance and efforts, rather than serendipity. Does talent and hard work help one in life? Surely. But I know a hell of a lot of talented, hard working people who haven't been destined to achieve the successes they've aspired to, many of whom have more talent and have put in more hours of work and study than people who rose to fame and fortune in business or the arts.

It's easy to spot the big, self-satisfied, egocentric types; stuffed shirts really, though I doubt they can recognize these qualities in themselves. I would venture that no matter how often a Donald Trump or a Henry Kissinger look in the mirror, all they can see is a reflection of *The Man I Love*, and can't imagine how preposterous they appear to anyone whose mind is not clouded by their wealth and social standing.

Effort, brains, and talent aside, I make the claim that it is all serendipitous; being in the right place at the right time under the right circumstances. Further, each serendipitous occurrence leads to another, and then still another, until, for better or for worse, we arrive at our present, though ever-changing, station in life. When it is "for better," this knowledge ought to make us more humble and more grateful.

It's 5:00 PM. March 19, 2004, the day before spring officially arrives. I'm sitting in my chair in a walled-in porch that serves as my office, with its corner to corner windows, looking out on a pristine, pastoral, snow-covered landscape My desk is cluttered with notes and letters, pens, scissors, white-out, and paperclips; all sorts of paperwork necessary to respond to, or to initiate, in order to keep *The Permanent Press* flowing. KPLU, my favorite radio station out of Seattle/Tacoma (www.kplu.org) is streaming the tastiest jazz imaginable on my computer's speakers. Maureen, who spent much of the day typesetting and filling orders, has just left for the day, off to East Hampton where she is a spinning instructor. Judy is upstairs, reading submissions in her office, which doubles as a guest room. Elise is working on her own writing projects at home, but we've had a phone conversation a half hour ago about submitting several of our books to a film producer.

All is right with my world at the moment ("Thank you Lord, for I did nothing to deserve this") and, as I think back on my own life, I can follow the string of occurrences that brought me to this happy point: publishing quality books with my wife, and working with Maureen and Elise D'Haene. I'd like to share these serendipitous moments with you, as well as tell you more about the world of publishing.

I won't bother going back to birth, childhood, adolescence, or my years as a young adult, though innumerable serendipitous events set the stage for things to come. Obvious things, common to all, like the fusing of one of my father's particular sperm cells with one of my mother's eggs. No credit to me for this genetic code. Or being born in the U.S.A. to a middle class family that could guarantee a roof over my head, food in my belly, and the opportunity to have a decent education. Best of all was having an incredibly loving and supportive father. These fortunate events, and then some that were incredibly painful at the time (like having my first marriage fall apart, being drummed out of psychoanalytic training due to my writings, and, later on, being censured by New York State Medical authorities), I now consider "gifts" for they all formed part of the pattern that brought me to where I sit today. They are already recorded in *The Reluctant Exhibitionist*, as I mentioned in my Introduction. So let me fast-forward to how Judy and I began our careers as book publishers and how, by grace of God, Fate, Destiny or Serendipity, we managed to survive.

**Serendipitous encounter #1: Frances Miller**

In 1974 I was under incredible pressure. There were childcare and alimony payments owed to my first wife, Eivor, from whom I had separated four years earlier, and there were obligations to provide some support for Judy and her three children, who now lived with me. The pressure came because I no longer had any joy in my work, yet needed this work to keep the money coming in. Being a consulting psychiatrist for the New York City Department of Corrections and the Board of Education had run its course. There was nothing more I could learn from it, nor any chance to be creative by initiating new programs. I had already explored many different therapeutic approaches, from individual psychoanalysis to group therapy, Gestalt therapy, Psychodrama, Rational-Emotive therapy, Rolfing, Guided Fantasy, and a dozen more. A year earlier *Peter Wyden* published *The Do-It- Yourself Psychotherapy Book*, my attempt to distill the common elements in all the major approaches to mental health and lay out a program where people could work on themselves. I felt burnt-out as a psychotherapist, for I had studied techniques from all the major therapeutic schools designed to help people and had listened to enough variations of the same stories that I was suffering from listening fatigue. Writing books for major publishers brought in a reasonable bit of money, though not enough to keep these two families afloat. Other than needing the extra income that a psychiatric practice brought in, clearly it was time to leave the field. But how could I do this with my financial obligations?

Judy and I, and our combined family of six kids, were on summer vacation at my house on Jobs Lane in Bridgehampton. Days were spent writing my first novel and tenth book, *A Question of Values* for *Dutton* (currently in print, with us, as *The Seducers*), writing longhand at the beach and typing up what I'd written in the afternoons. As sunset approached I'd relax by smoking a joint and bring my conga onto the deck to drum. Other days, when I finished work, I'd put one of several Barry White LPs or *Saturday Night Fever* on the phonograph and whirl and twirl and dance away until some level of ecstasy or exhaustion set in. These sunset routines were mind-clearing and meditative, and I wanted company with whom to share it. So I put a sign in front of my house, *Drum and Dance Adepts Welcome*. And into my life came Frances Miller, who lived in a beach house on Dune Road, and had heard the drums beating regularly. She came by, played drums with me and introduced Judy and me to Gene and Dorothy Friedman, whom she felt would be up for something like this. They, in turn, brought in others. Soon we were having drumming and dancing pot-luck dinners, in rotating houses, with a wonderful group of people: eating terrific food, getting a buzz on wine or grass, bonding and experiencing the joy of making music together.

Frances and I became close friends. Historically, we could not have been less alike. For starters, she was 81 and

I was a lad of 40. She was born, in 1893, into privilege; her family had one home on Fifth Avenue and an estate in Southampton. Her childhood featured governesses, trips abroad, schools in Europe, and "coming-out" parties, whereas I was born into a middle class family, went to public schools, and the only parties thrown for me were on my birthday.

At 18 she married a socially prominent Wall Street broker, raised three children, divorced 15 years later (in 1933, a year before I was born), only to be reborn, achieving prominence as an avant-garde textile designer. From then on she lived a life as an explorer, for Frances delighted in learning and doing new things, convention be damned. In 1948 she visited Haiti and fell in love with one of the natives. She brought him back to New York City, married him in a City Hall ceremony, and they went out to her Dune Road cottage to live. Imagine the shock and gossip this engendered: a white woman to the manor born marrying a black Haitian. But Frances could not have cared less. They moved to Mexico where she embarked on a second career as a painter. However, she soon left husband number two, who had a drinking problem, and returned to the Hamptons to stay.

Six-foot tall, Frances was a radiant, thoughtful, person with an inquiring mind and an impish mischievousness, who was always forthright if you asked for her opinions and, as should be clear, someone willing to disregard social convention in order to be true to herself. In this way we were alike, though our styles varied considerably. Frances was genteel, spoke kindly though frankly, whereas I could be brusque in my honesty and not nearly as sensitive to other people's feelings. She also had an intuitive ability to "do the right thing" for a friend in need, even when need was not directly expressed.

My summer was filled with writing, music, dance, and wrestling with the pressure of what I might do next to free my spirit from the harness of servitude brought on by my responsibilities to others. The Labor Day weekend was upon us and friends were visiting. We were due to depart on Monday to Nyack; our friends to their apartment in Manhattan. The kids had to go back to school, I to my jobs and my practice. It would be sad leaving, for my best times were spent in Bridgehampton. The sky, the greenery, the pristine beaches, the crisp air, the ability to write (all my previous books were written during these summer breaks), and having free time to walk, dance, play, made my soul soar. Dropping a tab of LSD on Sunday afternoon, I wandered down to the beach, in the hope of finding some relief and some answers.

Enlightenment came tumbling out of the heavens, an idea I never would have conceived of on my own: "Stay put and don't move back. Anyone from either family is welcome to live with you and you can guarantee a roof over their heads and food on the table." I also realized that this news would be a shocker and I was not ready to head straight back home to announce this position. I was still tripping, the sun was lowering in the sky, and I started to get goose pimples. Being on the beach, near Frances' house, I headed up her ramp and walked in, uninvited, to a cocktail party she was having for some older friends, clad only in my bikini. Frances, seeing me, never missed a beat. With a welcoming smile—and no explanation from me—she ushered me into her crowded living room, draped a blanket around me for warmth, patted me on the head, and told me to stay as long as I wanted. It was done with no more significance than letting the cat in out of the rain. And so I simply sat on the floor for I don't know how long.

When I returned home I told Judy and our friends I wasn't going back and made my offer to Judy. There was much consternation. "What to do with the house in Nyack?" "Sell it, whatever you want to do." My friends thought I had lost my mind, and I suppose I did lose a piece of it; the part that said you had to keep things running smoothly even if the smoothness was smothering. I also phoned Eivor, my ex-wife, and made the same proposal, for I had to escape these obligations that kept me imprisoned, work-wise, while offering safe harbor to the others for whom I cared. As it worked out, Eivor would have none of it and decided that she wanted to go back to Norway, while Judy, God bless her, came to my rescue by supporting a move out here, though after a week of living apart it seemed more practical that we wind things down that fall, close out respective jobs, sell our Nyack house, and move to the Hamptons full time the following spring. There I hoped to support myself by writing, for it was the spot where the Muse came calling me.

We finally moved out full time in 1975. Ironically, I never wrote another book from scratch, although I did do a major revision of *Dying* in 2000. Until now.

Cut to 1977. It's an early winter day. Frances phones to ask if I would drive her to a printer, Jed Claus, in Mattituck on the North Fork of Long Island. She's in the process of meeting with him after having completed her memoir, *"Tanty": Encounters with the Past.* In 1972 she'd broken her hip and, during her recovery, unable to stand up and paint, she embarked on this writing project. Three years later she pieced together parts of it for a *New York Magazine* short story competition and, as a finalist, her story was published in their May 2, 1975 issue. Several New York publishers contacted her after that, but none offered her a contract. Still, she continued to write and was now about to self-publish. "You'll like meeting Jed," she told me. "He's a very interesting man." And indeed he was, for besides printing books for others, he also had his own publishing company.

On the drive she asked me how things were going. I told her I was having my own frustrations; that New York State authorities were after me for writing my erotic memoir, now years out of print, and I could not get any of my previous publishers to reissue it.

"Why bother with them any longer," she asked. "Why not do what I'm doing and publish it yourself?"

Thus did Frances deliver the idea for *The Permanent Press*.

It turned out to be a very felicitous concept, because it also appealed to Judy, who has had a life-long passion for books. At that time our income was being generated by finding a desirable piece of land in the Hamptons, where an acre near the beach could be purchased for $20,000, taking out a building loan, moving into the completed house, then putting it on the market or renting it until it was sold. It was also Frances Miller who encouraged me to become my own architect. "Decide what rooms you want, what they should look out onto, and then drape a shell around them." And that is how I began; making cardboard models, having a draftsman draw up plans, and then supervising the construction. Judy, despite her input, was not as enamored of this work, though I was enjoying the creativity of designing and building. Searching for a buzz of her own, she would leave during the week, going to New York to resume her acting career, while I built and watched the kids. But we missed one another. So when the concept of becoming publishers arrived, it was enticing. Judy would read and help shape manuscripts and we could spend our time together and with our family without interruption.

We complemented one another well as business partners: she going over 90% of the submission we received (today about 6,000 each year from which we select 12), passing on to me the books she liked, and my giving those a second reading. If we were both in accord, we'd publish; if not we'd pass. Our tastes turned out to be similar. It was rare, if one was passionate about a book, that the other would not enjoy it as well. Judy assumed the primary editorial role, while I was engaged in everything else: production, art direction, networking, promotion, weight-lifting (unloading cartons of books that came from our printer or came back as returns from bookstores), and supervising an office staff of one or two part timers for the next quarter century. This was a job that suited my needs. Medicine and psychiatry eventually got boring, but this work was multifaceted. There were always new challenges to face, new people to meet, new books to promote and work to do that was in the service of the arts.

### Serendipitous encounters #2 and #3: Gary Hoffman and Thomas Lask

I don't remember which book it was, but one of my publishers, back in the 70s, had booked me on Bill Boggs' mid-day television show in New York to promote it. That's when I first met Gary Hoffman, Boggs' producer. Gary was a sweetie: bright, young, warm, open-faced, and very hospitable. Though I've lost contact with him over the years, (he moved to California to pursue his career as a film producer, while his lovely wife, Julie Carmen pursued hers an actress), we became good friends.

One spring day in 1978, Gary invited us to their place in the country where we met another author who had written a bestseller, *The Supercops*. We got to talking books and bitching about our various publishers who we felt could never do enough for us, a familiar conversation among authors. Now that I'm a publisher I see things differently and bitch about the lowering of cultural standards so that a lot of crap is promoted and sold while books of quality usually go begging. I complained about my first book, co-written with Marjorie Lee, G*ames Analysts Play*, that *Putnam* published in 1970. "They'd send me out to different sites to do a book tour. I'd be booked on a couple of TV and radio shows in Cleveland or Pittsburgh, and there would be no books in the bookstores! How ridiculous is that? And when they ran low on copies, they waited before doing a second printing, The result being that *Games* had a major book review in *The New York Times*, but no new copies would be available for another four weeks."

This author's complaint was that the non-fiction book he wrote, an even better book than *The Supercops*, about Mike Quill, head of the New York City Transit Workers Union, had come and gone in an instant, with few sales to its credit. "You would think something could be done about it," he said.

"Surely," I answered. "You'd think that some publisher would be bright enough to repackage it with a cover emblazoned with *By the Best-selling author of The Supercops*."

Then, when we finished complaining about our publishers, we got down to discussing the fate of good books that went out of print, a thought dear to all writers. That's how the concept of *Second Chance Press* was born, a rather grandiose scheme considering that were just releasing our first *Permanent Press* books, had no effective way of distributing them to the public (other than taking copies of *Seascapes*—a communal coffee-table book of Judy's poems, hand written by Deedee Topham, designed by Pam Topham, and with photographs taken by Rameshwar Das—and my book, *The Reluctant Exhibitionist*, to stores in the Hamptons). The result was that we distributed fewer than 200 copies and actually had sales of half that amount.

If you are not in the book business, know this: it is not only bizarre, but a publisher's nightmare. Why? Because you can "sell" a book to a bookstore, but the bookstore can return all unsold copies back to you for credit. In truth, every sale is really a "consignment," not a true sale until a buyer purchases a copy of the book at the bookstore. This is unlike any other business, for car manufacturers don't take cars back that are unsold by dealers, food packagers don't take back foods unsold in supermarkets, hardware stores can't return hardware to the manufacturer, and on and on ad infinitum. You can be out-of stock for a book, order more copies from the printer, send out back orders, and a month later get all these second printing copies back along with a good deal of your first printing. As one wag put it, the story of books sales is "Sold today, returned tomorrow." Another thing to be aware of is the superinflation of sales figures regularly claimed by publishers. When the public is told "100,000 copies sold," it can usually be assumed that the real number is half that amount. Then, given returns that can be sent back for several years, perhaps 25,000 copies are actually sold. Yet, this is the way books are hyped, the way a "buzz" is created, and the way bestsellers are coaxed into being. Like lemmings, people want to read what everybody else is reading.

To launch this next enterprise, I wrote a letter to the Authors Guild, asking if they would inform their members that we were establishing *Second Chance Press* and were looking to bring back into print good books that went out-of-print prematurely. (In the marketplace, books have a shorter shelf life than milk does at the corner grocers. With approximately 50,000 plus books published each year, and shelf space remaining constant, stores must clear out the old to make way for the new. Thus, books that have scant sales are returned to publishers to make way for new releases. The publishers, with limited warehouse space, have only two options with these returns: remaindering them (selling them for 25 cents to a dollar or two, *if* they are lucky, so that they can be put on the bargain basement shelves of bookstores or discount stores) or destroying them, if they are not so fortunate. The result is that most books go out-of-print in less than three years from first publication.)

We decided to do things differently, feeling that if a book was good enough to publish in the first place, it was good enough to keep in print. We also promised to keep our books in print as long as we published; our commitment being made not to "what's new" but to "what's good."

Imagine our surprise when we opened the *New York Times Book Review* a month later and read Thomas Lask's *End Papers* column, which appeared regularly back then. Somehow, he had picked up on the Authors Guild letter and printed it, giving our address. To our even greater surprise, we were sent 600 books over the next month. Judy and I chose 6 books from these submissions and our second imprint was to be launched in the fall of 1979 with the publication of Charles O'Neal's *Three Wishes for Jamie*, Haywood Hale Broun's *A Studied Madness*, Julian Schuman's *China: An Uncensored Look*, Richard Lortz's *The Valdepeñas*, Mitch Goodman's *The End of It*, and Dola DeJong's *The Field*.

We had it made, I thought. These books were better than anything I might write, and if I could get $30,000 to write a book based on a proposal, these six, on merit, should make us rich. I went to the Bridgehampton National Bank, told them all this, asked for a loan, and was rejected. They were a lot smarter than we were. Maybe one of the loan officers knew something about the book business that we had yet to learn. Or, perhaps, they simply intuited it.

**Serendipitous encounter #4: Howard Graham**

I started playing tennis at Sag Harbor's Mashashimuet Park back in 1970, and one of the guys I played with was Howard (Bud) Graham, who was the president of *Franklin Watts*, a mid-sized publishing company in Manhattan that was known for publishing school and library books for children and had produced the first large-print books for adults. I told him about the Lask column, the new imprint we were starting, and how we were operating by the seat of our pants since we had no real plan as to how we would get our books out to the trade. As it turned out, he liked the *Second Chance Press* concept and, as luck would have it, his company had decided to enter the adult book market ("adult books" was not a euphemism, back in the '70s for books of sexual content, but simply meant books for grown-ups). They were coming out with a list of six books to start with, mostly non-fiction, and if Judy and I were interested, they'd carry our titles (five of them novels) and so have 12 books to start with, as well as the two *Permanent Press* books we were bringing out. In short, they'd be our distributors.

*Franklin Watts* would take a 25% commission on sales, warehouse and ship all of our books, and do all the necessary paperwork and collections. Plus, they'd pay us monthly, the month after shipping. It was an offer we couldn't refuse, for now there was a sales staff to represent our titles to bookstores and wholesalers, and the fast payment to us would enable us to meet printing bills. This would give us both access and legitimacy. Howard's offer to distribute was also quite generous, as I was to learn, for other distributors would take 28%, charge additional percentages for handling returned books, and not disburse funds until three months or more after books were "sold," a formula guaranteed to prevent any profit and likely to eventually push one into bankruptcy.

Hallelujah!

## Serendipitous encounters #5, 6, and 7: Arthur Ceppos, Nat Sobel, and Richard Gallen

Though we had gained credibility and began garnering good reviews for our books, there was still no profit to be had. We were financing ourselves on credit cards and barely making ends meet. Arthur Ceppos had been the publisher of *Julian Press* (and later advised *Penthouse*'s Bob Guccione of *Penthouse Press*), and I first came into contact with Art when I was writing books and articles. Art was a very helpful and knowledgeable guy, and it was his *Julian Press* contract that we first adopted for use with our authors. One night, a few years after we started, he and his wife Pru had us to their Greenwich Village apartment for dinner, where we met the agent Nat Sobel, a friend of theirs. As to be expected, we talked about books, the book business, and our struggle to make ends meet. During our conversations, Nat decided that it would be good for us to meet Richard Gallen, who was working on a tax shelter that might be helpful to us. It would turn out that Richard would become our greatest benefactor.

Richard, when I first met him at his Fifth Avenue offices, was imposing: a well-dressed, soft-spoken six-footer who never separated his eyes from mine. I knew in advance from Nat that he was both a lawyer and an entrepreneur, and I could see that he was sizing me up. He introduced me to his elderly, yet still debonair father, Milton, also a lawyer, who worked for him part time. There was an obvious love between the two men, a good sign, for I had felt so similarly about my Dad. You sensed Richard could immediately separate straight-talkers from bullshitters and good investments from bad ones. He had a long history of investments, involvements, and business dealings in the arts. At one time he acquired Hal Roach studios and sold that film company three years later. Most of his work, though was in the book industry. Richard had been general counsel to *Dell* and *Grove* publishing, invested in several start-up publishing companies, packaged and published books on his own, and was one of the original partners in *Publishers Group West*, a distributor that carried many smaller presses. He talked about the tax-shelter he'd recently set up with investors who would "buy" the printing plates for somewhere in the neighborhood of $3,000 per book, yet still enable participating publishers to print their books. Did we want to be one of the publishers who might benefit from this? Does a bear shit in the woods? Who would not welcome this? I never did understand how it all worked, but I happily agreed to sign up and, for the next couple of years, the bulk of our printing bills were safely covered. And that was just the start.

Richard and his wife visited us in the Hamptons and recognized that I had a good eye for buying prime real-estate and for building houses, though I had no remaining capital to keep doing it, since much of the money we made in this way simply covered living expenses or went back into book publishing (it would take seven years before we got out of the red and started turning a profit). So he proposed another irresistible partnership: I would find a suitable piece of land that he would purchase. That done, I'd design a house and do the general contracting while he'd get financing for building it. I'd then find a renter until we sold it, at which time Richard would get back his investment plus interest, after which we would share the profits. These earnings would enable Judy and me to retire the mortgage on our property and get us out of debt. We'd already eliminated car payments by finding good used cars. Now, we had no more mortgage payments. When you are fortunate enough to owe nothing to anyone, you find you can live on a lot less income than you needed before. A great weight lifted from my shoulders, and we were now able to publish whatever it was we enjoyed reading without worrying about making ends meet. It was a glorious feeling, this gift from Gallen.

**Serendipitous encounter #8: Judith Applebaum (followed by other *PW* editors, and Anne Larsen at *Kirkus*)**

After we started with Franklin Watts I learned a bit more about the business of selling and distributing books. There were sales conferences where, twice a year, over the course of two days, the national sales staff sat down with the editors who had five minutes to pitch each of the books they acquired or worked on. We had the same opportunity. It sounded like an important event: fire up the salespeople who would, in turn, fire up the bookstore buyers they called upon. The evening before our first conference I put in time rehearsing what I might say about each of our eight books, hoping to convince the sales force that these books were "solid gold."

Rarely, in my life, have I sat through such boredom. Nor was I the only one. Looking around the room I saw that the salesmen's eyes, after the first half hour, started to glaze over and, despite refills of coffee, some were at the point, just before lunch, of nodding off. Little wonder! What could one possibly say in five minutes that would galvanize anyone? Moreover, as time went on, every presentation sounded more or less alike. "This book is about a love affair between...." "This book is a beautifully written tale of three generations..." "This novel is an adventure set in Georgia in 1890..." Listen to a hundred of these and the only conclusion to draw is that sales conferences are rituals, and mummified rituals at that. I dreaded having to present our books, for I knew that there was nothing I could say that would galvanize anyone, other than "Read the damn book if you're going to sell it," which would not have gone over very well. One of the great benefits of having our own publishing company is that, having no salesmen, I will never have to sit through another sales conference.

How then did one sell books? Through reviews, of course. And what were the most important reviews? Not what you would think, at least on our level. Surely good reviews in big city newspapers like the *Chicago Tribune*, *Los Angeles Times*, and especially *The New York Times* would enhance a book's sale. While these are certainly helpful, it soon became apparent that the two most important reviews were the pre-publication reviews in publications the general public knows nothing about: *Publishers Weekly* and *Kirkus*. Librarians are the last bastion for preserving our cultural heritage, and good reviews in both *PW* and *Kirkus* (aided somewhat by those in *Booklist* and *Library Journal*) are what they look for before ordering. And with libraries, a sale is true sale. There are also the dwindling handful of literary and independent bookstores. Unfortunately, they account for only about 15% of sales, with the chains—the Barnes & Nobles, Daltons, Borders, Waldens, and Amazon.com—garnering the lion's share. Scoring well with these pre-pub reviewers would give us a base sale of close to 1,000 copies, far more sales than one would get from a much larger newspaper review. Here, too, though, the question of review space arose, for far more books were published than these pre-publication journals could cover.

Enter Judy Applebaum, who was the fiction editor at *Publishers Weekly* at the time. Though we had never met, she took a shine to what we were attempting to do, liked the books we had sent in, and covered almost every one of them, as did her successors, Sybil Steinberg and then Jeff Zaleski. Without this coverage we would have sold nothing at all, since nobody would know that our books were out in the marketplace. The same holds true for Anne Larsen, the editor at *Kirkus*, who has also given our books extensive coverage.

Without these eight plus serendipitous encounters we would never have gotten anywhere, and I wouldn't have this story to tell. There were also two great disappointments that turned out to be terrific gifts, for they led us into solvency.

**Serendipitous events #9 and #10: Being dumped**

After being distributed by Franklin Watts for three years, Howard Graham went up the *Grolier* corporate ladder (the parent company of *Franklin Watts*) and was replaced by Frank Gillette, no friend of ours. Within the year he informed us that we were out: there was not enough profit to be made by them. No best sellers, no very good sellers either. Plus they needed the warehouse space for their own books.

It put me in a bit of a panic, wondering what to do with all of our stock, and wondering how we would get books into the general distribution stream. Scrambling about, someone mentioned that I contact Lee Heiman, at *Golden Lee Books*, a distributor in Brooklyn who was opening additional warehouse space. We met, arranged for a trucking firm to take our inventory from *Watts* to *Golden Lee*, and contacted independent sales representatives to show our books nationwide, breathing a sigh of relief that we were able to make an eleventh hour adjustment. But it soon became apparent that there would be other problems in this arrangement: the biggest one being our salesmen. In addition to giving *Golden Lee* commissions for warehousing, shipping, and billing, we now had to give salesmen a 10% commission for orders they brought in. Worse still, these sales people had to be paid within a month of selling to bookstores, and many of them dropped us after a year or two, for the same reasons *Franklin Watts* did: not enough sales and not enough profit for them. Except that this was worse, inasmuch as they sold to a lot of stores that never paid us, and once they left we could not recover the commissions we paid for these bad accounts or for the returns made by the good accounts. All in all, we were probably now paying out over 30% for warehousing and sales fees and getting reams of print-outs every month in order to could keep track of our inventory and determine which authors got paid for what books. Two more years passed, losses still accumulating, when we got dumped for a second time. *Golden Lee* needed the space for more profitable books and we would have to make other arrangements.

This time around I decided to do something different. Instead of looking for outside space or hiring salespeople, we converted one of our outbuildings to a warehouse and took back all of our inventory. We also abandoned the idea of using salesmen. Instead, Judy and I went out to Sommerville, New Jersey, and sold directly to *Baker & Taylor*, the biggest library wholesaler in America. And I flew out to LaVergne, Tennessee to meet with the buyer at *Ingram*, the largest wholesaler to bookstores in the country. These two giants probably supply 80% of all independent bookstores and libraries, places that, as said, are likely to order because of good pre-publication reviews. (Bookstores would never spend time ordering directly from the thousands of individual publishers when they can go to *B&T* or *Ingram*, place one order, and get books from hundreds of different publishers.) And guess what? By giving up salesmen we lost no sales, had no bad debts, and stopped giving away 25 to 30 cents on every dollar taken in. That is how, after seven years, we finally became profitable.

Not only that, we didn't have to wade through reams of print-outs to see our inventory. A walk out back to eyeball the skids our books were stacked on told us just what we had. It also cut down on our workload. Another great relief! Then again, had we not stumbled on our present property, one of the most serendipitous of events, we would never have been able to do this at all.

All of these happenstances brought me into intimate touch with the old concepts of Destiny and Fate: that what you do in life is determined by forces outside of your control, that if the good Lord wants you to succeed at something, events occur that make it happen. Conversely, if you are not meant to succeed, these ostensible happenstances never occur at all. Or, as the Desiderata states, "Whether or not it is clear to you, no doubt the universe is unfolding as it should."

Many good things have continued to happen. Over the past 26 years we've published, and still have in print, nearly 300 books which have garnered over 50 literary honors. *The Permanent Press* itself has been cited three times for editorial excellence. In 1988, we were a Grand Prize Finalist for *The Boston Globe Literary Press Competition*. In 1997, we were honored by the *Small Press Center* for "having done much to advance the cause of small press publishing over a period of at least two decades." 1998 marked the culmination of prizes, as we won the equivalent of a publishing "Oscar" for the previous year's list: *Literary Market Place's LMP Award for Editorial Excellence*—a prize open to every publisher, large and small in America, and voted on, electronically, by our colleagues in the book industry.

Because we operate a "low overhead" press, we can afford to publish what we like to read, not what the largest common denominator likes to read. It costs us approximately $10,000 to launch a book, and we can break even by selling a thousand copies. Publishers who have big staffs and pay bigger advances (all of our contracts and advances are the same: a $1,000 advance against royalties), have to sell 10 times that number in order to cover costs.

We've also found many good friends in this business: agents, authors, and editors here and abroad who share our vision: people like Doris Engelke of *Eichborn Verlag* and Tom Schlueck, both in Germany, Lora Fountain in France, Jan Michael in the Netherlands, Jay Landesman, Bill Albert, and Jane Judd in England, Rita Vivian in Italy. And back in the USA, Howard and Karen Owen, in Richmond, John Keegan and Bill McCauley in Seattle, the itinerant Robert Wintner (formerly of Hawaii, then Seattle, then Santa Cruz, and now back in Hawaii again), Larry Duberstein in Cambridge, and Bruce Ducker in Denver, just to name a few.

But the greatest friend of all, perhaps, is Elise D'Haene who, when still living in Los Angeles sent us her manuscript, *Licking Our Wounds*, which had the most unforgettable opening paragraph of any book I've read:

> *"I just had a pitiful orgasm. It doesn't even qualify as full-fledged. Let's just call it an org. It was fast, less than a minute to cum, and before the first beat of the clitoral tom-tom sounded, tears were running down my cheeks. Emotional cumming. The ache was loss and as soon as I conjured up a picture of your sweet sweet face and*

*those moony eyes, well, all was lost. My vagina misses you too, like my heart, and both of us spilled forth, gushed tears and wet cum like two blubbering babies hungry for a nipple. What's the song say? I'm a whimpering, simpering child, romance finis, and all that shit."*

It was a book about a woman who "lost her vagina" after losing her lover, and her struggle to find it again. It was also about the scourge of AIDS that befell her men friends. Yet with all of this sadness there were moments of great humor.

After Judy and I read her manuscript we called her to tell her how wonderful it was. "But why did you send it to us, rather than to a gay or lesbian press?" Judy asked. "Well, first, I consider it literature, not a gay or lesbian book. And secondly, it's politically incorrect for gay publishers." What a perfect answer! We talked some more and it was love at first talk. When we published her novel in 1997, we were also planning a party to celebrate our 20 years of book publishing. We have four bedrooms in our house that we wanted to fill with authors we felt closest to. Elise and her partner, Celeste Gainey, were among the four we invited out for a weekend.

It turned out that Elise and I had a lot in common, aside from the fact that we both loved women. She had been a therapist, just as I had been. I wrote books earlier and Elise wrote screenplays. We shared a common irreverence. Also, the year we picked up the *LMP Editorial Award for Editorial Excellence*, *Licking Our Wounds* won the *Small Press Book Award* for the Best Gay or Lesbian Book of the Year and was selected for *Susie Bright's Best American Erotica* yearly collection.

A year later Elise and Celeste bought a house in the Springs and moved here year round starting in 2001. Both were looking for a change of scene, Elise being tired of grinding out screenplays to satisfy the marketplace and wanting time to work on her own writing. For several years I'd been concerned about how *The Permanent Press* might go on when we no longer could. Judy didn't exactly feel that way: "When you're dead, you're dead," was her basic response. I suppose a lot of this has to do with motherhood. She had 3 grown children and perhaps that was her creation and her legacy. I had two surviving kids, but didn't have to undergo nine-month pregnancies. But we had given birth to the publishing companies and I wanted them to survive us. I also felt an obligation to keep our books in print and to honor contracts for future books we'd signed up. But how to accomplish this? We tried several times to find a buyer among the larger publishers where we could continue working until we either headed into senility or the airplane went down with all aboard. Despite coming close, nothing ever happened. Grossing $300,000 a year wasn't appealing to any of them; one needed to pull in a million dollars at the very least to whet their appetites.

When Elise moved out here she came into the office part-time to both hang out and help us. What a treat that was, for she's a woman with a huge heart, a great sense of humor, excellent taste in books (meaning she likes the same type of writing that we do), and has a gift for communicating her enthusiasms to others. By the end of 2001 a light bulb went off above my head, a Eureka phenomenon. "Stop trying to sell the press to accountants. Elise, 25 years younger than us, is the person to pass the baton on to." Even better, she went for the idea and became our

Associate publisher.

The final serendipitous moment occurred when Elise's sister, Maureen, moved out here from Rhode Island in January 2003 to help Elise care for their dying mother. She had time during the days with nothing to do and Elise was spending less time in the office as she had started on a writing project of her own. We needed help in shipping books out, and so Elise sold "Mo" on the idea of coming in part time to help out. Just in time, too, as within months our assistant, who did a little bit of everything, including type setting, decided to leave for the West Coast, and Mo became a fixture, managing almost everything. She's a big-hearted, generous woman, bright and strong. This 42-year-old personal trainer can unload a truck faster than I can and completes us as a family affair: two Shepards and two D'Haenes a lovely arrangement replete with camaraderie.

So I say "Thank you God," for it is easier than saying "Thank you Serendipity," but it really means the same thing when you get right down to it. We owe our viability and what success we've had to all these chance encounters, as does everyone else on this earth.

*Serendipity*, a tune I wrote to provide a dose of reality, makes the argument for destiny and humility in less space than I've occupied in this chapter.

***Serendipity*** *was recorded in Virgin Gorda in February 2004. I sang and Marcus Mark did the arrangement and played all instruments.*

LOVE

## THE PERFECT LOVER

Love's the smile upon your face, and
Love's the warmth of your embrace, and
Love's the way you look at me with tenderness
and longing.

Love is our anticipation
For the deepest exploration
Of the hidden passages of body and of mind.

In my life I've known a lot of other loves
Though we would always drift apart.
Yet when I met you it was certain from the start
That we had gained each other's hearts, forever.

Love's the moments after passion,
Hearing sighs of satisfaction
Soft caresses, eyes locked in to
One another's souls.

Love's what makes me want to hold you
Kiss your lips as I enfold you
The most perfect lover
I have known.

# LOVE

*What is this Thing Called Love*—the lovely title of an old tune and a question that is asked again and again. "Do you love me?" "How do you love me?" "If you loved me you'd do (this, that, or the other thing)." There was a television show back in the '60s that featured celebrity guests and one of the questions, always asked as the interview ended was "How would you define love?" There were many responses, often interesting, yet all seemed circumscribed. Little wonder, when you think of it. Lao-tsu's classic *Tao Te Ching*, the most widely translated book in the world after the Bible, consists of 81 single page poem/chapters each of which touch on the nature of the Tao, the basic principle of the Universe, and how one might live in harmony with it. Again I quote from the $56^{th}$ poem which starts this way:

> *"Those who know don't talk.*
> *Those who talk don't know."*

This could be equally applied to Love. The problem in talking about love is that it's a *feeling*, not an *intellectual* conception. You know what love is when you feel it; it's nothing that needs to be taught or defined. Love flows from the heart, not the head, though one can provide all sorts of valid reasons, after the fact, as to why one loves somebody. I can tell you why I love my wife and my friends, and list all the sterling qualities that they possess. But stepping back, I can find these same qualities in people I do not love.

It's not my desire to discuss love of country, love of

God, love of chocolate (well, okay, maybe chocolate, but not here), for there are so many types of interpersonal love that warrant more attention, like love for friends, for parents, for children, for spouses, and for lovers. All of these loves subsume a quality of caring, support, concern, and affection. At times, these loves come into conflict with each other. Sometimes these loves fade away and disappear. When that happens, what is one to do?

I don't presume to have any ready answers. I suspect, as I type, that this monologue will produce more questions than answers. I can share my musings about love and describe some of the situations I've faced in my own attempt to honor love. I also hope to be able to talk about love as a process, one within a social setting. But before getting into the particulars, it's fair to state certain concepts and attitudes I've come to, the first being that, *in matters of love, friends are at least, and often more important than family.*

Despite all of the cultural reverence for family, for FAMILY UBER ALLES, you are not guaranteed the love and respect from them that a good and deep friendship provides. Sisters, brothers, parents, and children are biological accidents. They may cherish you or they may not. You may honor parents for giving you life, accept your siblings because of the long relationships you've had with them since birth, and care for your children as a noble responsibility. There may be "liking" or "disliking" thrown into that mix. A close friend of mine, when discussing his will, said, "I don't feel like I have to leave anything to my kids. I love them, but I don't really like them." Frankly, I'd prefer another term for this sort of parental love: where you *love* but don't *like*. I'd label it instinct, the maternal or paternal instinct. Love, in the way I use it, goes beyond tolerance. If you are fortunate enough to have family members who are also friends, who are people you would *choose as friends even if they were unrelated to you*, that is the truest blessing. I've had a few of these extraordinary kinships starting with my father, and for that I feel blessed. But I think this sort of love within the context of family is the exception, not the rule. With good friends, it is the rule.

## The Will: The choice of the biological or chosen family

For the past few weeks, Judy and I have been in conflict over the question of altering our wills. Once upon a time, having three children each, it was easy, and our first wills divided our estate among all six kids. When my son Yan died, I instructed that his share be divided amongst my two remaining sons, so they would be getting 50% more than Judy's children. But over time, and Judy's questioning that arrangement, we drew up will #2, dividing things equally among the remaining five children, and that will has been in place for several years. We were, after all, one family, and though the biological connections now favored her side, I felt relieved to find myself capable of giving up my own genetic favoritism.

Over the past half year though, I began to question my unexamined linkage of genetics and inheritance; the questions arising because of the circumstances of two of my closest friends, people I love dearly, Craig Braun, who I met 34 years ago—a year before I met Judy—and Maureen D'Haene, who I've known for a year and a half. Both have enriched my life and have opened my heart wider

I first met Craig back in 1970. He'd seen me on The

*David Susskind Show*, a popular evening television program where I was leading a group encounter, and he was impressed enough to call for an appointment. When he came to my office I asked some pretty basic questions and the picture that emerged was this: Craig was an independent designer and packager who did album covers and inserts for the biggest musical acts and their record companies, including The Beatles, The Rolling Stones, Cheech and Chong, The Who, Alice Cooper, and Led Zeppelin, to name just a few (his *Tommy* album, which The Who recorded with the London Symphony Orchestra, would win a Grammy in 1973 for Best Album Design). A tall, handsome, magnetic guy, it was easy to see why so many beautiful women vied for his attention, for this was something else he reported. I started identifying with Peter Sellers, who plays a psychiatrist in the film *What's New Pussycat?*. In the opening scene of the film a well heeled, debonair Peter O'Toole visits Sellers and complains that his problem is that he is besieged by dozens of gorgeous women. As soon as O'Toole leaves the office, Sellers throws a jealous fit. Would I, too?

Instead, I asked Craig why he came to see me, and he had a hard time coming up with an answer other than he saw me on the *Susskind Show*. It was soon clear though, that work, money, and women were not his problem. "So what is your problem?" I asked. Finally, he said, "I want to feel things." "What things?" "Anything," he answered and wondered if I could make him feel something. This was pretty vague and I didn't know what he was really asking me. "Passion? Pain? Love?" "Anything," he repeated.

I assured him I could definitely make him feel something, asked him to lie on the floor, on his back, pull his shirt up, close his eyes, and tell me when he *felt* something. When in position, I knelt down and bit his stomach. When there was no response, I bit harder. Still no response. I chomped harder still, and feared I'd break flesh, a junior Hannibal the Cannibal even before that book was written. In the end, I had to end my bite before he would acknowledge feeling pain.

It was an auspicious beginning and we talked at length about it. I saw Craig for many months as a psychiatrist, and then we simply became friends. More than friends. We became brothers, shared a lot of the ups and downs in our personal lives, counseled and were there for one another in times of stress, saw one another through separate divorces, and were sounding boards for the problems encountered on the bumpy road of fatherhood (and, for me, stepfatherhood as well). I used to joke that if Judy was my wife, Craig was my husband.

An orphan, raised in Chicago by an adoptive mother who loved him and a father who didn't, Craig had a lot of street smarts. As a young hustler, he sold books of dubious relevance to nuns for their libraries (does one do this going door to door or nunnery to nunnery? I never asked). Got married, had a son, divorced, and didn't do a very good job of parenting. Moved to New York where he made a go of things, had offices in Los Angeles, New York, and London. Despite his artistic success, the women, and the money rolling in, by his early thirties, when we started hanging out together, it was clear that his drinking and drugging were excessive. Wine and booze each evening and then cocaine to revive himself. His company collapsed. He nearly went to jail for tax evasion. Then, twenty-five years ago, he began to turn it all around by committing to Alcoholics Anonymous and learned to live without booze or drugs. With sobriety, the best came out in him. He married again, to a much younger woman, and had two more sons. When his wife left him, he weathered the storm. Always a very funny guy, he morphed into a very wise and caring person, a good son, and an involved and concerned father to his two youngest boys.

In March of '94, at the age of 54, he was still working on music packaging, this time designing CDs for *Time Warner*. He was a bit burnt out when a friend asked him what he'd be doing if he could choose his heart's desire, a fantasy question to be sure. Craig's answer was "An actor." "What's stopping you?" his friend retorted. The next day he had lunch with another old pal who retired from advertising and had become an actor. When Craig recounted this earlier conversation, this man referred him to someone from the Neighborhood Playhouse, another example of serendipity. Craig signed up for an acting class, worked hard at his craft, went to auditions, took early retirement from *Time Warner*, and then lost, through no fault of his own, 75% of his equity as *Time Warner* stock tumbled during the George W. Bush recession. So now he works at his heart's desire, but roles are hard to come by, he has no safety net, and the future is scarier and less secure than it was before.

Maureen's story is also one of starting over. One of 12 children, she came out to the East End from Rhode Island, as mentioned, to help care for her dying mother. While here, she came to realize that her marriage was one in name only. Nor was there any likelihood for improvement. It was a loveless union, emotionally and physically, and it had been that way for 18 years, though her dedication to her two teen-aged boys had helped obscure her situation. Like Craig, continuing to lead the life she was living provided a certain security, though it imprisoned her spirit, and, at age 42, she had a lot to make up for. So, without a job, a circle of friends, alimony, or a penny in the bank, she began crafting a new life for herself. A very bold endeavor indeed! A bright and beautiful person in every sense, direct and without agendas, she possesses a big, compassionate heart that she wears on her sleeve, along with a certain fragility that tests her many strengths. As with Craig, I was touched by her struggle. Here, too, where was her safety net?

And so I told Judy I wanted to write will #3, going back to six shares of our estate, treating all our kids equally with five shares for them, and leaving me free to spread the remaining wealth elsewhere. Why would I necessarily want to favor the nuclear family members when there is another family that I am equally and, in some ways, even closer to? Given the fact that two of my closest friends are teetering on the edge, financially—much more so than any of our children—why not provide for them? In fact, the more I thought about this, why not leave additional inheritances to friends whose finances *are* secure, just as our children's finances are secure. These musings made me feel expansive. Money is, in many ways, symbolic, and a gift of money—money you can't use after you've died—lets people know just how much you loved them. It's putting your money where your mouth is.

Judy did not welcome this idea. She felt that all assets should flow to family, including our seven grandchildren, and by this new provision I was taking away from all of them. She could accept my desire to share some of our assets with friends, but not such a large amount, preferring that the bulk of this sixth share should go to our biological family.

For my part, I argued that it was just and proper that

we each should control 50% of our estate, and that wills are living things, changeable as circumstances change. If she divided her share amongst her three children, and I divided mine equally amongst my two surviving sons and used my last third for the benefit of my friends, all the children would still have equal shares.

"Whatever you do with your 50% is up to you," I told her. "But this is what I want to do with my 50%."

It was one of those disputes not open to compromise.

One of the strengths of our marriage is that Judy and I are capable of stepping into one another's shoes (No, we're not cross dressers, though in 1988, on a visit to Boston to gather our awards in the *Boston Globe's Literary Press Competition*, I had to borrow a pair of her lacy, rose-colored bikini panties—since I don't wear underpants—in order to get into a whirlpool in the hotel's spa to relieve the pain of a severe backache. It was then that I came to truly appreciate the story of *The Emperor's New Clothes*). She was, bless her heart, somewhat understanding of the 50/50 concept and tried to appreciate my sentiments about my chosen family. However, giving up a substantial amount of money that would have flowed to our children and grandchildren has been difficult for her.

**Love and Expectations**

In his lifetime, Alan Watts, through his writings and lectures was the leading interpreter of Eastern religions to Western audiences. In his autobiographical *In My Own Way*, he describes the sort of marriage ceremonies he performed when friends asked him to wed them.

"What I am about to say may at first sound depressing and even cynical, but I think you will not find it so in practice. There are three things I would have you bear in mind. The first is that as you now behold one another, you are probably seeing each other at your best. All things disintegrate in time, and as the years go by you will tend to get worse rather than better. Do not, therefore, go into marriage with projects for improving each other. Growth may happen but it cannot be forced. The second has to do with emotional honesty. Never pretend to a love which you do not actually feel, for love is not ours to command. For the same reason, do not require love from your partner as a duty, for love given in that spirit doesn't ring true and gives no pleasure to the other. The third is that you do not so cling to one another as to commit mutual strangulation. You are not each other's chattels, and you must so trust your partner as to allow full freedom to be the being that he or she is. If you observe these things your marriage will have surer ground than can be afforded by any formal contract or promise, however solemn and legally binding."

Holding with an open hand is a prerequisite for a good marriage, civil union, or for couples simply living together. There is much less reason to flee from or abandon a mate who allows the freedom that Watts advises. While this sort of tolerance would seem to provide the best rule for maintaining a lasting relationship, it's not necessarily easy to achieve that state of equanimity. Many short-circuit their chance to get there by trying to limit their partner's activities and emotions. This sets up a warden/prisoner relationship, one not conducive to love.

Why do we fall into such traps?

I have no definitive answer, though various possibilities are easy to understand. Sometimes it has to do with one's need to control things. Often, it has to do with an unwillingness to wrestle the green monster of jealousy to the ground. Possessiveness, the desire to control, and jealousy seem to be built into our genetic code.

In the '60s, a lot of us worked on this. It was the era of testing the premises of authority and social mores. The theme of those years was "Make Love, not War." There was Woodstock, Flower Power, experiments with communal living, open marriages, and swinging. If passion led you to fuck another woman, though you knew it was not threatening your marriage, how could you deny your mate the freedom to fuck other men? Or woman, for that matter? When these things occurred, and they certainly happened to me and many of my friends, jealousy is the first emotion that comes up. But by allowing this openness to continue and living with it for a while, some of us got a better perspective on things, and learned to contain the harmful effects of jealousy by realizing that what is good for the goose is good for the gander. It then became possible to turn these negative reactions into something more positive, with the currents of anxiety being transformed into excitement.

**Love and Language**

I've often wondered if mutes who marry have more loving relationships than people who are capable of speech. Words can convey love, but they can also cause alienation. Mutes, who must communicate through touch, expression, and gesture, are spared the pain of seeing minor differences of opinion escalate into argument and recrimination. My own guess is that they have more harmonious marriages and friendships than folks who can talk. Who among us can't recall a perfectly fine time with a friend or mate when some minor difference of opinion escalated into unwelcome argument, as each participant tried to convince the other of his or her point-of-view while negating the point-of-view of the other party? Reasoning, in such cases, does not lead to consensus, but to divisiveness. Nikita Krushchev once quoted an old Russian saying: "Better to keep your mouth shut and have people think you are a fool, than open it and prove it." Talk can heal or lead to polarization. Polarization is not healing. Tranquil waters, not roiling seas, are what nourishes love.

**The Gifts of Love**

I've received so many gifts of love that it would take another book to list them all. But three stand out above the rest, for they each changed the course of my life.

*My father's gift was given in this context*:
I was 23 years old, in my first year of medical school, and engaged to be married to Brenda, but I was filled with dread. I'd actually met Brenda years before, when I was 19 and attending NYU. She was a precocious 16-year-old classmate of my sister at Queens College. It was a relationship where she seemed totally loving and adoring, wanting nothing more than for me to tell her that I loved her, too. At first I couldn't say this. But one fine day I

awoke and felt YES! I DO LOVE BRENDA, and I drove out to her house, certain she would rejoice on hearing this wonderful news. But when she got into my car she calmly told me that she'd just met someone else. "Sorry," she said "but it makes no sense for us to see each other anymore." I was undone by this, of course, drank myself to sleep that night, and went into a shell for over a month. Then, years later, while in medical school, I ran into her again in the lobby of a mid-town theater. She was leaving, I was entering, we both had dates. She was wearing a beautiful fur coat, looked stunning, smiled widely, and said "Marty." "Brenda," I beamed back. We exchanged phone numbers and soon were off and running.

It was total bliss at first. Great contact, great sex, great story-line: boy meets girl, boy loses girl, boy finds girl again, and they live happily ever after. So we got engaged. Her parents laid out some money and we planned a summer wedding, renting an apartment in Queens, buying furniture at Knoll's, and a beautiful, red, used MG-TD sports car. Wedding invitations were sent out and everyone seemed pleased with the coming union… except me. I felt an increasing sense of dread about our impending marriage though I couldn't say why any more than I could give voice to my misgivings. Still, I saw no way out. I didn't know what to do. How could I back out at this late date? What reasons would I give? How could I disappoint so many people? I didn't feel I could even talk about it with anyone. What I did know is that I felt trapped, not happy, like a man under sentence.

A week before the wedding I was visiting my folks. Standing outside, reading my mind and my soul, my Dad came up to me, put his arm around my shoulders, and said "Marty, I just want you to know that if you have any doubts about this wedding, don't feel you have to go through with it for my sake or anyone else's." It was like the weight of the world was lifted from my back. I was so grateful and close to tears for this relief. It freed me to get up the courage to phone Brenda and tell her that the wedding would not take place (another twist on the story-line, when boy, after reuniting with girl, leaves her and lives happily ever after). This was one of the many great gifts my father gave me.

*The second loving gift that changed my life came from Chris Thompson.*

I was married to Eivor, but our marriage was deteriorating badly. We had, on the surface, a good life: a beautiful old house in Grandview, Rockland County, New York off Route 9W, overlooking the Hudson River, with terraced lawns, a swimming pool, three young children, and a summer home in Bridgehampton. Yet, she was bitter about many things, including the strains that an open marriage caused her. Plus she was drinking. Each night, when I came home, it was to an inhospitable house and a cold, cold bed. This had been going on for over a year, despite the fact that I had given up outside intimacies for a good stretch of that time, yet never objected to her exercising this freedom.

Chris was a lovely woman, a former Eileen Ford model, and possessed an IQ that was, I'm sure, stratospheric (having an uncanny memory she once claimed to have been "born to play Trivial Pursuit"). I knew her from my involvement with a growth center I co-founded, Anthos, in New York. She had been the girlfriend of Steve Gelman who led groups with us, and even after their break-up Chris stayed about the center. Then, one day she gave me her gift of love: herself.

When I got home that night and received my usual icy reception, I lay in bed. With a hostile stranger on the other side of me, I began to seriously question what I was doing there. The difference between lying down with Chris and sharing a bed with Eivor was so striking that I came to my senses very abruptly. My first separation followed. Although Eivor and I got together again after I spent the following week sleeping in my office (alone, for the record), this realization eventually enabled me to leave a broken marriage that could not be fixed.

*The gift of Judy*

I met Judy when I was 36. She lived on the third floor of an apartment building at 12 West 96th Street. I had an office on the 13th floor. A few years before that, I rang her bell while working on our dump-Johnson campaign—trying to pack the West Side Democratic Club with insurgents in order to pass a resolution denouncing Lyndon Johnson and vowing not to support him in his quest for renomination. It was the briefest of meetings, but I was struck by how attractive this five foot two (and, yes, eyes of blue) woman was. An actress, she was married, with three kids. That was the last contact I had with her for the next several years. Except for one instance twelve months earlier when we were both heading into the building at the same time. I asked what she did. She said she was working as a drama therapist with psychiatric patients at The Mount Sinai Hospital in a program she and a friend started. I invited her up to my office to continue the conversation, but in the back of my mind I was hoping to make a pass, for she had lost none of her luster. But "shiver me timbers," as the pirates say, there was no opportunity to do so. Our conversation was so proper, with no flirtatiousness on her part, that making any sort of pass seemed inappropriate.

Several months of attempted reconciliation with Eivor followed my intimacy with Chris. I forswore other women but, paradoxically, Eivor's scorn increased. Did she see this as a sign of weakness? Was it the result of too much drinking? Or payback time? Or was it some accident of genetics, for her mother had numerous shock treatments and crazed episodes in the past? I couldn't figure out the reasons, but I certainly saw that time was not healing this wound. One night, on going to bed, she really let me have it. "You're too weak to leave me," she snarled. "Just a little Jewish boy who's too tied to his mama." Well, that certainly did it. I couldn't possibly let that pass and have any self-respect left. So I got out of bed, packed a small suitcase, and drove to my office, planning on staying there indefinitely.

I asked the elevator operator about "the woman on the third floor." "Didn't you know? She and her husband split up a couple of years ago." So I called her at 10:30 at night, asked if she remembered me…the shrink on the 13$^{th}$ floor. I told her I was taking a vacation from my wife, asked if she was free the next night, and said I'd like to see her. "Sure," she answered.

Our first date began in a very pedestrian way, devoid of atmosphere or romance. We attended a tenants meeting to discuss the landlord's attempt to turn the building into a cooperative. We sat through that meeting, listening to tedious discussions, and when it ended I sought something more intimate and took her to a neighborhood bar for a drink.

During a lull in the conversation, she asked what I was thinking and I answered truthfully. "I was wondering what you looked like with your clothes off." "Why in the world would you ever think that?" she asked. I must say I was dumbfounded by her response, for why wouldn't a lot of guys think this, sitting across from an attractive and intelligent woman? The upshot of this evening was that we saw each other continually from that day forward. I soon did get to see her with her clothes off, and within weeks moved into her small apartment, which included her three kids, two dogs, a cat, gerbils, and other assorted wildlife.

Judy has given me so many gifts. Her ability to mostly hold me with an open hand, her willingness and judiciousness in helping raise my children, her being my partner and best friend through three decades, her "Never Say No" approach to intimacy; her ability to put herself in another's shoes and see things from my side when we'd have disputations, her encouragement to live out my dreams, as in giving up security for creativity, or moving to the Hamptons—all these gifts of love, displayed over so many years, have altered my life profoundly.

**Pure Love**

Back in the 1970's I was invited to a seminar being held in Bucks County, Pennsylvania, where I was on a panel with Ram Dass, known earlier as Richard Alpert who, along with Timothy Leary, did pioneer research with LSD at Harvard University. It was shortly after his book *Be Here Now* was published. The discussion revolved about self-realization, and it was pretty clear that Ram Dass was a fully realized person. What do I mean by that? Simply that when you were around him, either seeing him with others or talking to him yourself, you had the feeling that he was *right there with you; connected as deeply with you as possible.* The openness of his face, his gaze, his willingness to listen, his simple direct responses (which could also be unpretentiously profound), represented, for me, the purest form of love. I use the term "purest form," because he offered perfect acceptance without having any apparent agendas or needs that he wanted you to fulfill.

A few years later, I went to see Swami Muktananda during one of his visits to the United States. Muktananda was a widely respected guru from India and his followers arranged a reception and luncheon for him in upper Manhattan. I traveled up with Leon, a patient of mine that I took on from a city-run clinic, a middle-aged guy who was out-of-work and inching ever closer to psychosis. He had a lot of rage and was sometimes on the verge of losing it. Yet, he also seemed to be striving to put his past behind him. That past included his having been a hit-man for the mob. Leon was a man of keen intelligence, very well-read, largely self-educated, and could quote Nietzsche and Kant. Certainly he was not your typical ex-mobster. I thought that Leon might find something at this meeting that could be helpful to him.

There were at least two hundred people in attendance. After eating some Eastern food (guru/health food, you might call it) we all entered a large auditorium, took seats on the floor and listened to Muktananda's short introductory remarks, emphasizing compassion, stillness, and nonviolence, following which he took questions. One devotee complained that he had embarked on several spiritual paths, going from guru to guru, but never arriving where he wanted to be. Muktananda listened, just as openly as Ram Dass listened, and told him a story about an Indian farmer whose irrigation system was drying up. He dug several wells, all twenty feet down, but each one came up dry. Desperate, he finally asked advice of the village wise man who told him it would better to dig just one hole and keep going deeper until he hit water, which the farmer eventually did at thirty feet. Another student then asked him about death, and what it meant to him, in the course of which the Swami told her that he believed death was simply a transition and that he had no fear of it.

At that point Leon got up, walked over to Muktananda, sat in front of him and, agitated and almost frothing at the mouth, challenged him, saying, in his staccato, Brooklyn-accented voice: "You say you're not afraid to die. Yeah? You sure? I wonder how you'd feel if I was to pull out a pistol right now, point it in your face, and tell you 'Time's up'?" I was aghast. I knew that Leon owned a pistol. Could he have brought it with him? Have I so misread this man that I could be facilitating an assassination?

Muktananda's response was incredibly disarming. He locked eyes with Leon and with compassion and a soft smile said that he might feel a moment of shock, but that this might just be the way that he was supposed to go, and we all must die sometime. His voice and composure was like an embrace, with no fear, no anger, and no panic. Leon suddenly dropped his challenge, thanked him, arose, and came back to join me.

Muktananda's warm sincerity, this "being right with you in the here and now," is another example of what I would call *perfect love*. It also explains why tens of thousands of people have loved him and certain other gurus, for reverence inspires a reciprocating reverence. Nor are these qualities limited to swamis or gurus: it's just that, by reasons of reputations, more people know about them. My Dad was as "realized" as either of these two men, yet he worked at being an artist, not as a spiritual leader. Those dozens of people who came in close contact with him surely adored and respected him as much as the masses who followed Ram Dass, or Muktananda, or the Dalai Lama. The same might be said for Hans van de Bovenkamp. I'd met Hans a few years ago at a local book fair to benefit the Southampton College library. He was wandering the aisles, talking to various local authors, and came over to visit me. A Dutchman and a phenomenally good sculptor, he too possessed these same qualities: an openness, a radiant smile, and a way of "just being there with you" when you talked to him. It was a case of love at first sight.

Speaking of the Dalai Lama, a half dozen years back Judy and I watched a Public Television Network feature on him, admiring his simple honesty, openness, decency, and warmth. The following week we saw another show about Yogi Berra. As soon as it was over, we looked at each other and said, "Yogi and the Dalai Lama seem exactly alike," for they both displayed the same qualities. The moral of these stories is, *You don't need a huge following to be a fully realized person and an inspiration to others.*

One last guru story: this one about Chögyam Trungpa Rinpoche, who brought Tibetan Buddhist teachings to the West in a unique and unorthodox way, who was the guiding light for the Naropa Institute (now called Naropa University) in Boulder, Colorado, and who founded more than 100 meditation centers.

About thirty years ago I flew to Boulder to attend a play writing workshop given by Jean Claude van Itallie. I was attempting to write a screenplay and thought this admired playwright had much to teach me. At that time, Rinpoche was visitng Naropa and in the evening several thousand students, acolytes, and the curious assembled to hear him speak, myself among them. I'd never seen him before and knew him only through vague word-of-mouth. His talk that night was about the need to look within, not without, for guidance, and the trap of looking up to a guru. I could easily identify with that for I was increasingly troubled by the respect I received when leading psychological groups. My words were so often hung on to, at times reverentially, when other members of the group could say things that were even more astute, but were not taken in, for these others weren't the "leader." How does one get out of that conundrum?

While Rinpoche was speaking he was also drinking from a cup, and his words became ever more slurred. After his brief talk, as with Muktananda, questions were taken. Most were respectful, none of them touching on the reality that the guru was getting drunk in public. At the end of the questions, Rinpoche had to be helped off the stage as he could not walk under his own power. One woman, sitting next to me, said it was quite terrible that he would do that in this setting. My response was quite different. I thought it was perfect, for he was living what he was teaching, demonstrating by his unconventional conduct, the message of all good Masters: don't blindly follow your guru, but go deeper into yourself in order to find your ultimate spiritual answers.

One last story if I may, concerning my own attempt to deal with the problem of excessive respect for the "leader." This came about on the last workshop I ever gave, long after I stopped working as a psychotherapist, but I had committed myself nearly a year earlier to lead a weekend group at a growth center in Massachusetts that would focus on group process, leadership, and self-discovery. As fate would have it, Marco Vassi, a good friend, perhaps the best erotic writer of our generation (Saul Bellow, Norman Mailer, Kate Millet, and other heavyweight novelists all sang his praises), and a guy who frequently lectured at Anthos, had come out to Sag Harbor to visit Judy and me. We'd already reprinted 11 of his books and also published two of his original titles: *The Other Hand Clapping* and *A Driving Passion*. The thing about Marco was that his stories were often extensions and elaborations of his own robust sexual life. Raised a Catholic, he threw off the yoke of repression and plunged into the world of sexuality head first, having relations with thousands of men and women alike. Funny, charming, philosophical, playful, and dramatic, he was a practitioner of Tantric Yoga: enlightenment through sexual experiences.

In any event, I asked him on a Thursday afternoon if he'd like to accompany me to this workshop, for I was feeling totally burned out and bored after working in the field for 10 years. His answer was "Beautiful." As we drove up to the center the next morning, after sharing a joint in the car, an idea dawned on me to which he readily agreed. We would switch identities—though I insisted on getting the choice room reserved for the group leader.

That evening we met with the ten participants and Marco, as "Marty," suggested we all introduce ourselves and say something about what we were looking for. Following this he asked everyone to close their eyes and slowly struck a gong ten times as he encouraged everyone to relax their bodies and clear their minds. Then he boldly announced that he was retiring to his room, would be available for consultations throughout the weekend and, in the meantime, we should conduct our own group since there were several people in the helping professions in attendance. With that he left and you can imagine the uproar that followed.

"What is he doing?"... "This is outrageous!"... "I paid good money to see Dr. Shepard work, and this is what he does?" My response, as "Marco," was to say "Fuck him. We're intelligent people. Let's see what we can do without him." And we were off and running.

I had never felt so involved in a group in years. I was revitalized, listening carefully, trying to be helpful, pushing things along. But I could also see that I was not being taken any more seriously than anyone else in the group. Then, on Sunday morning, at our last session (which Marco attended), we came clean. One or two people had suspicions of what was going on, the others did not. One of the most dissatisfied participants was a psychologist who felt "gypped" and wanted her money back. She paid for Martin Shepard and got Marco Vassi, and could not come to terms with the fact that I was in that group the entire time, working as well as I had ever worked in my life. Fortunately others gained something more positive from this experience.

(I share this afterthought. It turned out that one woman, a therapist herself, had visited Marco in his room after dinner on Saturday and told him that the main reason she attended this workshop was because, having read my books and becoming a fan of mine, she hoped she might be able to give him, Marty Shepard, a blow job. While the real Marty Shepard would have refused, as I found her unappealing, the ever open-to-experience Marco said, "Be my guest." After achieving her goal she drove back to her home in New Hampshire that night and never attended the Sunday session. I realized, with some embarrassment, that this woman would likely add to my checkered reputation this intimacy that I never participated in.)

## Jealousy and gossip as They Impact Love

Jealousy doesn't need a sexual component: just a feeling that "*I* am losing something because *you* are so involved with someone else." I know that in the past I've been jealous of Judy when I have seen her getting so involved with the lives of her grown children. I can attest that this emotion is potentially poisonous, both to the one that feels it and the one who is under scrutiny. And is anyone immune from the effects of gossip? Not me certainly, though I do make a show of pretending I am and plowing ahead, for I refuse to lead a circumscribed life because of the opinions of others.

Possessiveness, jealousy and gossip are as much a part of the human heart as is love. While many, including myself, have tried to disarm these responses with varying degrees of success, one could just as easily argue, "Why bother if it's a natural response?"

For myself, I know that if I were not willing to rise above the fear of gossip, I would not have lived the rich and rewarding life I've led. I've also come to believe that trying to limit the flow of love your significant other feels is not the healthiest of responses, for it imposes burdens on those who demand it and places chains around those of whom it's demanded. It's an anti-life move.

Should one reign in their affection for another person because a mate feels threatened? Does loving others mean you love your mate any less? I think not. When partners fall into these traps it puts great strains on a relationship, and that's a sad state of affairs indeed.

Yet these situations occur with frequency and highlight the difficulties of love in practice, as opposed to theory. That difficulty has to do with exclusivity: the confusion that arises when you find yourself having loving feelings for more than one person. Or the despair that one's mate or lover feels should he or she learn that you feel that way. To my way of thinking, these reactions, even if innate and sincerely felt, are logically absurd. Love is an exalted state that enriches, for it's the best response that human beings are capable of. Should not love then, be allowed to flow freely, spread widely, and not be dammed up, bottled, or restricted so that it can only be expressed toward individuals A or B or C? *What the World Needs Now is Love Sweet Love*—another apt song- and limiting your potential to love others does not make the world a better place in which to live.

I would hope that you who read this will not be browbeaten when someone you love becomes jealous of someone else you love, for feelings of love are a gift that falls from the heavens into our hearts, a gift that should not be returned to the Sender. It commands us to open our hearts to love, not to suppress it. Can a woman love two men, or two women, or a man and a woman? Can one love two or three, or a dozen other human beings regardless of sex, family connections, and marital status? Certainly so. One has to believe this deeply in order to contend with the "one-size-fits-all" myth of their being only "one person in the world for me," or only one conventional way of loving. A wider belief in love is necessary to enlarge your own vision and tolerance when you feel threatened by your mate or when your mate feels threatened by you. It can help to reign in your pain, possessiveness, and anger, or enable you to resist being intimidated by your lover's pain, possessiveness, and anger, depending on which side of the equations you find yourself.

These are my beliefs and thoughts about love. The more important questions is, "What are yours?"

**The Perfect Lover**

Before his death, John Houston was asked in an interview what gave him the most satisfaction in his illustrious life. His answer, to paraphrase, had nothing to do with his accomplishments as an actor or film director. Instead, he said his greatest pleasure was "that so many lovely women lowered their knickers for me." A few words, then, about the deepest, most compelling love: the sort of love where one is just so happy to be in the company of another, to touch, hold, caress, take care of, and protect that person. The sort of love where one's heart is full and brimming over, and where a person wants to thank God or fate or their lucky stars for providing this extraordinary feeling.

*Love is a Many Splendored Thing*, as another golden oldie says, and being intrigued by its many forms, I decided to write a ballad about Love. Being that it raises a host of questions, I opted to focus on one particular type of love that should be familiar to many, the sublime satisfaction felt when in the arms of your beloved. *The Perfect Lover* is my attempt to describe that particular state . How long does the perfect lover remain that way is not for me to say. With Houston, it was a renewable resource. For others, when finally found, it lasts a lifetime.

**The Perfect Lover** *was recorded in Virgin Gorda in February 2004. I sang while Marcus Mark played all instruments.*

# HOME

***Home*** *was recorded in Virgin Gorda in February 2004. I played saxophone and Marcus Mark played everything else.*

## HOME

"Home," to me, is a place of great security, one that gives rise to feelings of warmth and gratitude. It's a place in the heart, a place beyond reason, a state of restfulness and comfort were the heart is overflowing with feelings of safety and love. At the end of the day, it's the place you want to visit; a state of peacefulness, tranquility, transcendence.

It's certainly beyond words: a state of mind in which words disappear. As said in so many other words, my father, Mac Shepard, was the most remarkable and loving man I've ever know. He was a quiet guy with a good sense of humor, a great listener, a man of great tolerance and compassion, a wise man, largely self-educated, who offered opinions only when asked and was always there to give a warm embrace. He was a good artist and, for the last several years, his subway sketches have adorned both the front and back cover of *The Permanent Press*'s catalog. Mac was rarely critical and invariably supportive and loving toward me no matter how often I stumbled or how far outside the traditional social boundaries I sailed. He taught me that "Everybody is always doing the best they can," and that teaching has helped me see the world through others' eyes even when my attitudes and perceptions differ from theirs. Unconditional love is what I always felt Mac gave me, and I loved him dearly in return.

He died of colon cancer when he was 64. My sons Marc and Richard were 7 and 6 at the time, and my biggest regret was that they couldn't have known him longer.

Mac figured prominently in two of my books, *The Reluctant Exhibitionist* and *Dying: A Guide to Helping & Coping*, and that book is dedicated to him, for we spent much time together during the last year of his life, with me taking countless photographs of him, which he watched me do with an amused yet warm detachment, knowing I wanted these memories after he'd passed on.

A dozen or so years ago I blew up several copies of a favorite photo I took and framed them, putting one in my house and another in my studio. It's akin to others putting up pictures of their gurus. In truth, Mac was mine.

Every time I look at his picture, see his face, and look into his eyes, I am Home.

When I am in my lover's arms, I am Home.

When I see a beautiful sunset, or share tenderness with a good friend, I am Home.

When I look at my dogs and they look back at me, I am Home.

Songs can bring me Home, as when I hear Bill Evans play the piano, Miles Davis play the trumpet, or John Coltrane play his sax. So soulful, all of them.

But words alone will never do the notion of Home justice. Words can dance around it, but the state is an emotional one, far better conveyed by music than by talk. So I end this book with this short chapter, and my shortest song. Hopefully, you can share my sense of Home by listening to this final, wordless tune.